# WOLF BOUND

## LUNAR ACADEMY, YEAR ONE

### ALYSSA ROSE IVY
### JENNIFER SNYDER

# WOLF BOUND, YEAR ONE

## LUNAR ACADEMY

**Alyssa Rose Ivy**
**Jennifer Snyder**

# GLOW

"Ouch." I rubbed my shoulder from where it somehow managed to make contact with the doorframe. Okay, the reason for it wasn't so mysterious; I'd been too focused on my phone to notice where I was walking. To be fair, I wasn't texting or doing anything frivolous. I was reading the latest articles in Warlock Updates. Truthfully, I never got much from reading the journal, but one never knew when something would surprise them.

"Hey, you okay?" Lionel Daniels stood just inside the entrance to the Wolf Bound dorm. He wore an amused expression that made his hazel eyes look even brighter than normal. Not that I knew how bright his eyes were normally.

"Uh, yeah. Fine." I gave a terse smile and headed for the stairs. In another life, I would have loved the attention from Lionel. I would have loved any attention from Lionel, but this wasn't another life. This was my life.

"You sure? It looks like your shoulder took quite a hit." He followed alongside me.

I stopped and looked over at him. "I'm fine. Okay?"

"Okay." He put his hands in the back pockets of his uniform pants. "But maybe next time put your phone away before walking through a doorway."

"Yeah. Sure," I mumbled as I made my way up the last of the first set of stairs.

Thankfully, he didn't follow. The guy was hot. There was no question about that, but he was also a distraction. I couldn't handle any distractions.

I pocketed my phone before I made my way up to the fourth floor. I didn't need to run into anything else, or attract more attention. Everyone in my dorm already knew what I was—or rather what I wasn't. I didn't need to give them any more of a reason to notice me.

"Hey, Glow." Penny looked away from her computer when I came in. Thankfully, my first roommate had requested a change, and I'd ended up living with someone who could at least stomach living with someone like me, a failure when it came to magic.

"Hey." I dropped my bag on the floor. "What are you working on?"

"Oh, just Wolf Lore homework."

"Fun." I took a seat at my desk and turned on my computer screen. I was one of the few students in my dorm who used a desktop, but I liked writing notes by hand, so I didn't need a computer I could bring places with me. I already stuck out like a sore thumb in Wolf Bound; there was no reason to stop there.

"How were your classes? Going to be okay this term?" What she was really asking was whether I was going to pass the magic classes. I appreciated her attempt to sugarcoat things, but it was unnecessary.

"I'll be okay." I loosened my tie and took it off. I was done with class for the day, which meant I didn't need to stay in uniform. I didn't mind the white shirt and skirt, but the tie had gotten old after the first few days. "I think."

Penny folded her hands in her lap. "You know I'll help you in any way I can."

"Thanks, Pen, but this isn't the kind of thing anyone can help me with."

"You have the abilities... you have to." Despite her words of encouragement, there was doubt in her eyes. I was sure she had no idea she was letting it show.

I shrugged. "I should. I mean I've showed the initial signs, but the whole late onset idea is starting to seem less likely." I wasn't the first wolf-witch hybrid to get her magic late, but there had only been a handful throughout history to get them past age eighteen, and my nineteenth birthday was fast approaching.

"But entirely possible. I've been doing some research and—"

"Hey." I stopped her before she could get too far in. "I appreciate it, I really do, but just because one or two wolf-warlocks and witches have gotten their powers as young adults doesn't mean I will."

"But it doesn't mean you won't." She turned around in her chair so she was facing toward my desk.

I did the same thing. "I should probably try to apply to Wolf Born. I know they'll say no— but it's the next logical step for me. I don't belong in Wolf Bound no matter what my potential is. It's time for me to accept it." I was generally a realist, but I was choosing to hold onto this fantasy longer than normal.

"But you can't leave Lunar Academy." Penny put her hands on my shoulders. "You are too good."

"Too bad there isn't a house for wolves that don't fit anywhere." Lunar Academy needed a miscellaneous house. "Maybe they could call it Wolf Misfits."

She cracked a smile. "There should be another house, but maybe they could choose another name..."

She was being supportive, but her words still stung. Even Penny, my closest friend at school, was admitting I didn't really belong anywhere.

"But there isn't. We know Wolf Born won't think I'm pure line enough. I'm not a vampire, so I can't join Wolf Blood. And I wasn't bitten..."

"We are going to find a way to get your magic out. I'm not giving in to any other possibility." Penny ran a hand through her perfectly smooth black hair, fixing imaginary knots.

"If there's any possibility I'm going to find it." It wasn't as if I wasn't trying. I'd read every book and article I could get my hands on. Hence how I managed to walk into a door frame.

"Good. Stay positive." She patted my shoulder before moving her hands back to her lap.

"I'll do my best."

"Any luck on the job front?" Penny switched to yet another of my less than favorite topics.

"Possibly." Not exactly luck, but ideas. "I have a few more places to look."

"Good." She turned back to her computer. "I have to finish this paper, but how about we grab dinner as soon as I'm done?"

"Sounds great." I opened my Charms & Enchantments book. I wasn't really hungry. I was too stressed to be hungry. Yet I'd eat because one needed to eat. Just like I'd study because I needed to study. My life was becoming a series of doing things because I had to not because I wanted to do them. I was close to full-on panic mode, but I didn't panic. I always managed to stay calm under pressure.

I tried to focus on the words on the page, but they all started to blur together. "I'll meet you at dinner. How much more time do you need?"

"Maybe forty-five minutes?" Penny glanced up. "Everything okay?"

"Yeah. I just need to check out a job thing. I can't focus."

"If you need to borrow a little bit..." She didn't look at me when she made the offer.

"No. Don't worry about it." I shook my head. "I need more than a bit, so it's better that I find a job."

"You have such a good attitude." Penny smiled. "It's inspiring, really."

"I try." I grabbed my bag and headed back out again

down the hall and out into the common area that connected the first-year girls' and boys' halls.

I walked past a group of girls talking, but I headed straight for the stairs. I knew how they felt about me, and I wasn't one to sit around and make small talk to pretend.

The night was brisk in the most wonderful sort of way. January in the south wasn't like January in Pennsylvania, where I was raised. I didn't have to worry about ice and snow, but the chill in the air was welcome. Summer in the south was an entirely different experience.

I left campus with a quick glance over my shoulder. It was a quiet night, with only a handful of people walking between the dorms and the dining hall.

I headed down the main street and cut through the gas station, where one lone car refueled. I nodded in greeting to the woman at the pump before pulling open the door to

Convenience. Not a particularly creative name for a gas station store, but it said everything it needed to say.

There was no one at the counter when I walked in, so I started to walk between the shelves of the store. It was all the usual stuff you'd expect to find in a store attached to a gas station. Snacks, snacks, and more snacks. Well, with a few things like hand sanitizer and magazines thrown in. And of course, there were the glass cases full of water, soda, and beer. Lots of beer.

"Can I help you?"

I turned away from the beer case at the sound of the male voice. "Hi, Mr. Wayes?"

"That is my name."

"Hi. My name is Glo—Gloria." I figured using my given name was more appropriate when job seeking. "I'm a student at the academy, and I was hoping I might be able to get a job with you."

"A job?" Mr. Wayes rested his chin in his hand. "And what house did you say you were in?"

"I didn't say, but I'm in Wolf Bound." What I didn't say was how short-lived my time in the house would probably be.

A small smile spread across his face. "I was in Wolf Bound."

"Really?" I knew this. Of course I knew this. That was why I was standing there asking for a job.

"You a first year?" He let his arm fall to his side.

"Yeah. I just started second semester."

He nodded. "It gets easier. It really does."

"Thanks." Although, I doubted it was going to get easier for me. One needed to be able to wield magic for that to be the case.

"You sure you have time for a job?" He turned his head from one side to the other as if he was studying me.

I tried not to let his appraisal make me nervous. "I need one." Hopefully he wouldn't ask too many questions, but I'd answer them as needed.

"The only shift I have open is the night shift. It's going to mean being here pretty late." He turned his head back over to the right side. "Sometimes even overnight."

"That's fine." Maybe I'd regret taking that kind of position, but I was desperate. It wasn't just the money. It was also access to Mr. Wayes. My research had involved looking for any help I could find.

"Really?" He seemed to study me. "You are Wolf Bound. That means finding a job should be easy."

"I want a regular job. You know." I really hoped he bought the line I was selling.

"And you're lying to me."

"I'm—" Was it even worth trying to defend myself when he was totally right?

"But I don't care." He shrugged. "You can have your secrets for now. You're hired."

"You don't even know my last name."

"I was in Wolf Bound too, Gloria Mayor. I know exactly who you are." He winked before walking toward the back of the store.

"Wait. Do I need to fill anything out? When do I start?"

"When do you want to start?" He glanced at me over his shoulder.

"As soon as possible." I didn't have time to waste.

"Then start tonight."

"Tonight?" Had I heard him right.

"Yes. Unless that's going to be a problem?" He ran a hand through his graying short hair.

"No. No problem at all."

"Good. I'll see you then." He disappeared through the doorway.

I headed back outside, hoping I hadn't just made a huge mistake.

# LIONEL

"$\mathcal{D}$o you understand the severity of the situation?" Professor Tyler watched me from across the huge wooden desk. It seemed excessively big, which probably meant it was making up for something else.

"Yes. I am keenly aware that this situation sucks." I tried to find a comfortable spot in the hard, strangely shaped chair. I was sure the choice of chair wasn't an accident either.

"Language." Professor Tyler glared.

"Sorry. It is unfortunate." I preferred my first choice of words personally.

"It is more than unfortunate, Mr. Daniels."

Yes. It sucked. But I wouldn't push it and say it again. "I am well aware."

"Are you aware?" He leaned over the desk. "Are you aware of what this means for you?"

"I am aware that this puts me in a bad position. Yes."

A shitty position was more like it, but bad was the more appropriate word choice.

"We will not expel you."

"Considering I haven't personally violated any policies, I'd hope not." I'd be using words far worse than sucks if they tried to kick me out of the academy.

"But your father made some considerable violations." Professor Tyler shuffled papers around on his desk.

"I am well aware." And I was getting increasingly tired of this circular conversation.

"We have decided that, given the circumstances, you will be stripped of your ability to use magic. Your professors will have discretion to give you temporary access to your magic for an examination or other educational purpose, but otherwise you will have no ability to use it …"

"Wait." I sat up in the chair. My back was hurting from it anyway. "You can't be serious. You can't strip me of my magic. I can already only use it in class. What does it matter?"

"We have to be careful."

I was pissed. Seriously pissed. "Why? What have I done to make that necessary?"

"You know we have to keep you on a short leash until your father's trial is over."

"Why? Because my sperm donor decides to dishonor our people, I can't use magic." I didn't care if I came across as disrespectful. That was all my father was to me. I barely knew the man, and now he was going to screw up my life? Not happening.

"Rules are rules, Mr. Daniels. You might as well learn now."

"There has to be some sort of appeal process. Something I can do." I was grasping at straws, but I didn't care.

"After the trial is over. Right now, there is nothing to appeal."

"Nothing to appeal?" I could almost feel my eyes bugging out. "You are restricting my rights."

"You are a student. You have no rights." He leaned back in his much more comfortable-looking chair.

I bristled. "Of course I have rights."

"You have the right to leave the academy. If that's what you want, I won't stop you, but I can't promise we'll hold a place for you."

"I'm not leaving the academy." I'd worked my whole life to get to this point. My mom had sacrificed everything to help me scrape up the money. I wasn't giving that up. "I will abide by your rules."

"Very well. We will set up a time to put the magic block on."

"Fine. I understand." I stood up. Anything I added would just hurt my cause, and I couldn't afford that.

Professor Tyler stood. "If it's any consolation, I am sorry you have found yourself in this position, Mr. Daniels."

It wasn't a consolation, but there was no reason to tell him that. "Thank you, sir." If he was surprised by my attitude's about-face, he didn't show it.

I walked out of his office and gave a brief nod to the receptionist before stepping out onto the quad. It was slightly cool out, but I always ran warm, so it didn't bother me. I wasn't normally a winter guy, but this year I was. It matched my mood after finding out the ridiculous things my father had done.

I glanced at my watch. If I hurried, I could still grab something to eat in the dining hall before it closed.

"Hey, man." I nearly walked into my friend, Keeton, as I entered the dining hall.

"Hey." He loosened his tie. "Where have you been? I waited for you in the lounge, but you never came back, so I gave up and ate."

"I had to meet with Professor Tyler."

"About that stuff?"

"Yeah, about that stuff." If stuff meant my father screwing up my whole life.

"Go okay?" He rubbed the back of his neck. He was nervous for me.

I looked around to make sure no one was listening. "I can't use magic unless it's for class."

"What the hell?" Keeton's expression darkened. "You can't be serious."

"Yeah, well I am." Too damn serious.

"What are you going to do?"

"What can I do? Follow their rules until I figure out a new plan." And I would come up with a new plan.

"That sucks, man. It really sucks."

"Trust me. I know that all too well." But talking about it wasn't going to change a damn thing. "I'm going to go in and eat before they shut down."

"I can go with you."

"Didn't you just eat?"

"Yeah, but that doesn't mean I can't eat something else."

"Whatever you say." I walked inside and started loading up my tray. That was when I saw her out of the corner of my eye. Gloria Mayer. She must have redone the tips of her brown hair because the purple was even brighter.

"Are you ever going to ask her out?" Keeton loaded his tray. How the guy could eat a whole second dinner—because I was quite sure he'd already had plenty—and not look it, I'd never understand.

"Glow isn't the kind of girl you just ask out." I watched her while trying to make it seem like I wasn't.

"Uh, what the hell does that even mean?"

"It means I can't just ask her out."

We moved to an empty table. "Or it means you are too chicken to ask her out. Big difference."

"I'm not chicken. I just know it's not going to go well if I just go up to her."

"Why not?" Keeton piled fried chicken on his plate. "You are a chicken, man. Just admit it."

"I've asked out plenty of girls. You know that."

"Then why is she different?" He grabbed a bowl of pudding. "The magic thing? Is that what this is about?"

"Of course not. Why would that matter at all?"

"I don't know... because she's probably going to get kicked out of school soon." He took a seat at one of the many empty tables. Whether purposely or not, he picked the side that allowed me to sit across from him and still

13

look at her. I sounded like a freaking stalker, but I didn't care.

"Well, I may be too." I took my seat.

"No, you are not. You're not leaving. Just don't use magic for anything but class."

"Easy for you to say." Keeton wouldn't last a day without using magic.

"I'd keep my cool and play along if I had to. Besides, how long do you really have to wait?"

"At least until the trial is over." However long that was.

"Have they even set a date yet?"

"No." I took a bite of chicken. "So I have no freaking clue."

"You'll figure it out. You always do."

"I kind of have to."

"Glow!" Penny ran across the dining hall, her heels clanking in the process. "I'm so sorry. I fell asleep."

Glow looked up from her tray. "It's fine. I was late anyway."

"It's not okay. I totally dropped the ball."

"Penny, it's fine. Now go get some food before they stop serving." Glow pointed to where the food stations were starting to go dark. Glow was so low drama. I loved that about her. So many girls would have been mad at their friend—or wouldn't have been cool eating alone—but she didn't even seem miffed.

Keeton glanced over his shoulder. "She is hot."

"Shut up," I snapped.

"What?"

"You know exactly what I mean. Don't be an asshole."

"I'm not an asshole."

"Then why would you say that?" My chicken no longer looked appetizing.

"I'm merely pointing out the obvious. The obvious that everyone sees. There's only one reason that girl is single."

"Yes. Because she's not the kind of girl you just ask out."

"Because she's going to get kicked out."

"Let's stop talking and eat." Lost appetite or not, I could eat.

A few minutes later, Glow and Penny got up and walked toward our table.

Penny leaned over, pressing her palms into the back of a chair. "You guys going to Morrison's party tonight?"

"Maybe." Keeton sipped his drink; it was probably sweet tea, knowing him. "Not sure if it's going to be worth the effort."

"I can't." Glow took a step back from the table. "But you guys have fun."

"Why can't you go?" Maybe it was none of my business, but I couldn't help but ask.

"I've got work." Glow took some of her purple ends and examined them. "Speaking of which. I need to go get ready. See you, guys." She half waved before running off.

"I should go with her." Penny looked between us. "But maybe I'll see you guys at Morrison's?"

"Where does she work?" I blurted out.

Penny wrinkled her brow. "Why do you care?"

"Just curious." I tried to play off my interest.

"You aren't trying to help get her out of here faster, are you?" Penny glanced at the door.

"Of course not!" Even the suggestion pissed me off. "If anything, it's the opposite."

"He wants her." Keeton smiled sheepishly.

I gave him a glare.

Penny laughed. "Ah. I see. Okay, then. She's working at Convenience. Night shift. I don't think it's a great idea, but she seems happy about it, and she needs to be happy about something."

I hated that. I hated that she wasn't happy. "Night shift can be hard."

"Uh-huh. I wouldn't sign up for it." Penny still wore an amused expression. "So, I had better catch up. Hope to see you guys later." She walked away.

"You are so lame, man." Keeton tossed a dinner roll at me.

I glanced around the mostly empty dining hall. "I've been accused of worse things."

"You're going to go see her, aren't you?" Keeton leaned back in his chair. "But you'll pretend you just needed to pick something up."

I'd thought about doing just that, but I'd also quickly rejected the idea. "Not tonight."

"Oh?" Keeton set down his empty cup. "You seemed very interested in her new job."

"Just making conversation."

"Right." Keeton grinned. "So what about Morrison's party?"

"What about it?" I was still trying to wrap my head around Glow working the night shift.

"If you aren't going to see Glow, then want to stop by the party?" Keeton pulled me partially from my thoughts.

"Maybe." I was already starting to backpedal on the whole not stopping by to see her thing.

"Suit yourself." He pushed his tray away.

"Always do." What I really wanted to do was go for a run—a run as my wolf—but I couldn't afford to break any academy rules. I could still run in my human form. "I think I'm going for a run. Not my wolf."

"I don't see why you get any enjoyment running as a human. It's boring."

"You know I'd prefer my wolf, but you can't always get what you want."

"Well, you could. But you can't be a chicken." He waggled his eyebrows.

Maybe I would stop by and visit Glow at work.

## GLOW

*I* wasn't entirely sure what I was supposed to wear to work, so I went with my winter fall-back. Jeans and a tank with a cardigan sweater. The tank was for when, without fail, the heat was on too high. I learned that trick back in high school. There were a few students in Convenience when I opened the door. They were upper levels I think from Wolf Born. They weren't in uniform, but by the arrogant way they pushed passed me, it was my best guess. They clearly weren't vamp, and they weren't from bound, and the arrogance knocked out bitten, so it had to be born. Sometimes, I wondered if my life would be easier if I'd been bitten. But my problems didn't stem from my wolf side. It was the magic that wouldn't show itself.

"Gloria, you came." Mr. Wayes helped the straggler from the group of girls check out.

"I said I'd be here. Did you really doubt I would?" Maybe he heard about my issues with magic and thought that meant I was unreliable. It couldn't have been further from the truth.

It wasn't until the door closed behind the last girl that he replied. "No, I didn't really doubt it, but you never know until the time comes what somebody will do."

"What would you like me to do?" I eyed the register. I assumed I'd be spending most of my time manning that.

"First, let me show you the back room." He walked around from behind the counter.

The hairs on the back of my neck prickled. It wasn't out of fear; I somehow knew I could trust Mr. Wayes. But I knew there was more than extra soda and chips back there. "Okay, great."

At first glance it really did look like any stock room. There were rows upon rows of boxes. Some were completely nondescript, while others had labels that hinted or flat out showed pictures of the contents. I tried not to stare at the box that held thousands of chocolate bars. I had a crazy sweet tooth.

"Come along. There is plenty to show you." Mr. Wayes didn't glance back to make sure I followed, but then again, he didn't need to. Chocolate lover or not, the candy wasn't what I'd come to see.

"How are you enjoying the academy so far?" he called as he turned down a small aisle. This back room seemed far bigger than it should have been based on how the building looked from the outside.

"Uh, it's been fine." Fine. Sure. Fine, if he meant did I enjoy the classes and was I glad to be there. Not fine, if he meant how school was going. I tried to hold off the panic, but I knew it was going to set in.

"Fine?" He glanced back at me. "That isn't how most would describe their first year."

Had I somehow put my foot in my mouth. "It isn't?"

"Most would describe it in one of two ways." He stopped and turned around to look at me. "Either they would describe it as eye opening and incredible, or they would describe it as stressful and dismal. I'm not sure how anyone would find the experience simply fine."

"Well. That's exactly how I describe it. It isn't awful, but it isn't great. It's somewhere in between."

"Any reason it isn't great?" His eyes were kind, and he seemed interested in my answer.

"Of course there is a reason. There is always a reason."

"True. There is. But then again, there is also usually a reason why someone doesn't want to share that reason."

"Wasn't there something you wanted to show me?"

"Yes." Mr. Wayes turned and continued down that aisle and then turned down another one. My original suspicion was right. This backroom was way too big. It must have been enlarged through some sort of magic.

"This area here is the restricted section." He pointed to a section of aisles that appeared darker than the others.

"Restricted from whom? It's my first day and you're already showing it to me. I assume customers aren't allowed back here."

"Restricted from those who do not wield magic."

I swallowed hard. I had to fess up. "Mr. Wayes, I should probably tell you—"

"You haven't come into your magic yet. I know."

"I turn nineteen soon... I'm kind of running out of time to suddenly get it, so you might not want me—"

"Gloria, you didn't take this job because you were looking to work at a convenience store."

"No." I wasn't going to lie. There was no point.

"Then you know who I am and what I'm capable of." He wasn't bragging; he was only saying it like it was. He was legendary on campus. He'd won Professor of the Year at least a dozen times when he used to teach, and even now that he wasn't in the classroom, he was still known as a powerful wolf. "And you know you can try your hand at magic under my supervision. By supervision I mean under my roof. I will not be breathing down your neck."

I NODDED. I wasn't sure what words to use. Sometimes nodding was the only thing to do.

"Then I take it you understand that I didn't hire you because I was desperate for a night cashier."

I shrugged. "I'm not entirely sure why you hired me, but I'm glad you did."

"I can feel the magic coursing through you. You just need to find a way to access it."

"And how do I find that way?" I'd tried everything. I'd spent hours upon hours pushing myself and studying.

Trying to surround myself with the best Wolf Bound had to offer.

"Only you know that."

"But I don't know it. I'm running out of ideas."

"One can never run out of ideas."

"Sure you can. It happens all the time." And not just to me. It couldn't just be me.

"If you are running out of ideas all the time, you have far bigger problems than not being able to wield magic."

"They are going to kick me out." I let the words fall from my lips. "I mean, I can apply to Wolf Born—they have taken a few hybrids over the years if their wolf parent had enough prestige- but I know that isn't likely."

"Do you want to stay?"

"Of course I want to stay. More than anything." I'd been waiting for my chance to attend Lunar Academy since I was a little girl. I was an only child, so I hadn't watched siblings go on ahead of me, but my parents told stories. And I read all the written accounts.

"Then you will find a way to stay. When we want something bad enough, we can usually make it happen."

"Usually. Not always."

"Usually is right. Focus on the positive."

"What's in this restricted section?" I glanced around. All I could see were boxes. These were smaller and none had labels, but on the surface, they didn't look particularly magical.

"You tell me." He threaded his fingers together.

"But I don't see anything."

"Did I tell you to look?" His eyes twinkled.

I thought about his words. "You mean feel."

I closed my eyes and reached out. I couldn't use magic, but I could feel it. And there was magic all over the place where we were.

"Okay, you've got it. I can tell. So open your eyes."

I opened my eyes. And all I saw were the boxes. "Am I supposed to see something now?"

"Yes." Mr. Wayes's brow furrowed. "You really don't see anything beyond the boxes?"

"No." I sighed. "Really, I don't know why I'm even trying. Maybe I shouldn't even take this job. I mean, they can throw me out any time after my birthday in April. I may not even be able to finish the semester."

"No one is throwing you out." He clenched his jaw. "Okay?"

"You don't know that."

"I do. I have some pull in Wolf Bound, you know?"

"Pull or not, you can't make them keep a non-magic in that house."

"You aren't a non-magic. You have plenty of magic in your blood. We just need to work on getting it out." Mr. Wayes glanced at his watch. "But unfortunately, that can't be tonight. I have an important meeting to attend. You are welcome to stay back here and practice that exercise. If you see what you're supposed to see, you'll know what to do."

"What about the store? Aren't I supposed to be at the desk?"

"No need for that. I'll have Jonathan take care of customers."

"Jonathan?" I repeated the name.

"Yes. The usual night clerk. He's a graduate student, but he was in Wolf Bound until a few years ago."

"Wait. I thought you said you needed someone for nights—"

"I also told you I didn't hire you to be the cashier..."

"Okay, then I'm guessing this job won't pay." Which was a problem, but not nearly as big of a problem as what would happen if I couldn't get my magic working soon.

"It will pay. You can do some organizational work for me, and Jonathan does need to take breaks sometimes. He'll come find you when he wants one. Until then, I suggest you practice here, or you can continue exploring this area. I do caution you from entering the aisles blocked off with red tape."

Red tape didn't sound particularly inviting, so I probably wouldn't have anyway, but now I needed to know why. "What's down those aisles?"

"Some of the darker sorts of magic. I can't stop you from going down them, but don't say I didn't warn you." With that, he walked off back the way we came.

I sighed. It was time to get down to business. I had no idea what I was supposed to be seeing, but I was determined to see it before Mr. Wayes got back.

I yawned. But first, I really needed a cup of coffee.

## LIONEL

*R*unning as a human was so much less satisfying than running as a wolf. I couldn't go nearly as fast, and it wasn't primal. But, even if my wolf was howling in anger and jealousy, it helped me burn off steam. The woods around campus were dense and deep. We all knew there were secrets buried all over, but that never kept me out. I could take care of myself. I tried to keep my head clear as a dodged trees, but my thoughts kept going back to Glow. Why would she have taken the job at Convenience? Was she trying to get to know Mr. Wayes? It was the only possibility that made sense. From what I knew of her, she wasn't rich by any stretch of the imagination, but if it was money she wanted, there were plenty of better places to get a job.

I smelled magic. A lot of it, and I followed the trail. It got stronger and stronger, and then it stopped. If I'd been in my wolf form, it would have been far easier for me to track, but shifting wasn't an option. I'd have to wait a few more weeks before I had the opportunity to run with the pack.

There was nothing to do about it. Although students shouldn't have been using magic in the woods, professors and staff could. There was probably a logical explanation for it. I reached out and touched the tree right next to where the trail stopped. It was warm, far warmer than normal. If I hadn't already sensed the magic, I would have known it then and there.

I looked around the area a few moments longer, touching other trees, picking up some dirt. Much of it was warm and held the tell-tale signs of magic, but there were no other clues. I ran back through the woods toward campus, but I didn't enter the dorm. Instead, I turned toward town.

I wasn't really going to go in to see her. I'd just run by the store because I wanted to extend my run. That was the only reason.

Of course, I couldn't even stay true to that. I ran back and forth down the main drag before stopping in front of Convenience. I pushed open the door.

Disappointed flooded me as I saw the guy sitting at the desk. "Hey, can I help you with something?"

"Uh, I thought a friend was working tonight. Sorry."

"You mean Gloria? The new girl?"

"Yeah." I hadn't heard anyone but professors call her Gloria, and that wasn't frequent since most used her last name.

"She's in the back."

"Can I go see her?"

"You're a bound?" He seemed to think about it. "Okay, then sure, but don't take anything. Mr. Wayes will be pissed at me if you do."

"I won't. I'm just here to see my friend."

Friend. I wouldn't exactly call her that. I mean we had classes together, and everyone in our year lived together inside a house and knew each other pretty well, but she kept mostly to herself.

I pushed open one of the swinging doors to the back room. I rubbed my eyes. The lights in this room seemed brighter than normal. Or maybe it was just me.

I didn't see her right off, and I debated what to do. How was I even going to explain why I was there? That was probably something I should have thought of before I came, but it was too late now.

I walked between two shelves lined with boxes. Mr. Wayes sure kept the shelves stocked. But then again, that kind of store probably went through a lot of food.

I sensed her. I'd always been unnaturally good at sensing other wolves, particularly those with magic. And she had magic. I didn't care what anyone said. She was loaded with magic.

I walked slowly as I grew closer. I took small steps as I felt her magic growing stronger and stronger. And then I saw her. She was standing with her arms stretched out and her eyes squeezed closed.

"Damn it." She sighed, but she didn't open her eyes. "I give up."

"Don't give up," I spoke without thinking.

Her eyes flew open, and she stared at me.

"Hey. Didn't mean to startle you."

"What are you doing here?" She licked her bottom lip, and my imagination went to what else I wanted her tongue to do. And what I wanted my tongue to do to her.

I hoped she couldn't tell how aroused I was. "I just thought I'd see how your first day of work was going."

"Are you always around when I embarrass myself?"

"What do you mean?" Had I missed something?

"I walked into a doorframe earlier. Now you caught me...well, doing something stupid."

"How is reaching for magic stupid? I'll give you the door thing might have been embarrassing, although you weren't the first person to do that."

"It's that I can't find the magic."

"But you feel it." I wasn't asking a question. I knew she could.

"Sure. It's kind of obvious."

"Not to everyone. You know not everyone can feel this low a level of magic."

"Low level? This isn't low level."

"It is." I walked down the aisle toward her. "You have far more magic in your veins than what is hidden in these shelves." And it was hot. Really hot. I'd never found a girl's magic hot before.

"What is hidden here? I need to know." There was real and true desperation in her voice, and I forced my less than pure thoughts away.

I was going to help her. There was no question about that. "I'm sure you can figure it out."

"I've been standing in the same spot for close to an hour now."

"Maybe that's the problem." I tried to put it as gently as possible, but it was kind of obvious to me.

"What is?"

"Standing in the same spot."

"Meaning I shouldn't stand, or I should move?"

Hopefully, she was good at taking direction and suggestions. "Maybe both. Figure out what works for you."

"Can't you just tell me what's here?"

"That would take away the fun, now wouldn't it?"

"Fun?" She raised an eyebrow. "There is nothing fun about this."

"Sure there is. Magic is always fun." I used my most exaggerated upbeat voice possible.

"Gee, thanks."

"Hey, put some work in and figure out your abilities, and you'll be doing more magic than me."

"Not likely. You're the best."

"I appreciate the sentiment, but not for long." I had almost forgotten she didn't know yet.

"What do you mean?"

I thought about what to say here. "Have you heard about the Pillar trial?"

"Yeah... the guy who exposed his identity to the human children in Savannah."

"Yeah, so that guy is my father."

She paled. "Sorry. I didn't know."

"I use my mom's last name. Easier that way."

"So, I take it he's had brushes with the wolf law before?"

"Yeah. That and the fact that he was never around."

"I'm sorry." Her eyes locked on mine. "I really am."

"Don't be. My mom more than made up for him."

"Still, you deserved better."

"How do you know what I deserve?" I kept our eyes locked. I couldn't pull myself from the brown pools.

"I'm generally a good judge of character."

"And you think I have good character?" That was officially the first compliment she'd paid me if she did.

"You do." She nodded. "No question."

"What makes you say that?"

"I just know."

"Okay. I'll let it go. I think you have good character too."

"Yeah?" She broke the eye contact.

"And lots of other good things."

"Is that so?" Her curiosity was piqued.

"You have a good smile."

"I hardly smile."

"Yeah, but when you do, it's amazing." It was contagious. It usually made me grin too.

"Amazing? That's different from good."

"It's better than good."

"Yeah." She looked away.

"I never knew you were shy."

"I'm not shy." She flinched as if I'd physically hurt her. Clearly, she didn't want to be called shy.

"Then, why can't you take a compliment?"

"I can take a compliment."

"You're beautiful, you know. It's not just your smile."

"Uh, thanks." She looked down. "Anyway, I'm sorry about your father, but where were you going with that conversation?"

I'd let her off the hook for the whole not being able to take a compliment. For now. "I haven't told many people, and I'd appreciate if you didn't broadcast this."

"I won't. I really only talk to Penny anyway, but I won't tell her if you don't want me to."

"Penny's going to find out. Penny finds out everything."

Glow laughed. "Yes. Yes, she does. She seems to be in the center of everything." I'd figured that out early on first semester. "And I don't mean that in a bad way. She isn't a busybody or anything."

"Yeah, I know what you mean. Besides, I'm not going to tell her what you said. Kind of works if we just agree everything we discuss here stays here."

"Okay, so everything that's discussed in the back room stays in the back room." Glow mimed a zipper over her lips.

"They stripped me of my use of magic. They put a block on that only a professor can take off when I need to use it in class," I spit out.

"Why?" Her brows knit together. "That makes no sense."

"Because my father used magic to expose himself. You know the archaic rules of families all being suspects when one member is brought to trial. I'm his son."

Her mouth fell open before her lips twisted into a frown. "I'm tired of the archaic rules."

"Yeah, that makes two of us."

"We should change them." Glow's eyes flashed.

"Change them?" I tried to follow.

"Yeah. I mean if we could change the rules, we'd both be in better shape."

"And how do you suppose we do that?" I was down with any plan she had.

"I don't know yet."

"I'm game if we do something else too."

"What?" She inclined her head to the side.

"Work on you wielding your magic."

"Why do you care about that?" She looked down.

"Because I know how badass you are going to be. I can't wait to see it."

She laughed. "Badass? Me?"

"You are the girl talking about changing rules that are hundreds of years old."

"Okay, when you put it that way, it is pretty badass." She grinned.

"Now are you going to take my advice?"

"What advice?" she asked.

"Glow." Had she really forgotten already?

"The one about not having to stand in the same place?"

"Yes. That advice."

"Okay. So what else do you suggest?"

"What seems comfortable to you?" She needed to

direct things. I could help, but only she knew what she needed. I knew what I needed. Her.

She walked over to the farthest edge of the aisle and sat down with her legs crossed. She leaned back against the shelf. "Truthfully, this."

"Great. Try it."

"Turn around." She spun her finger.

"Turn around? Why?"

"Because I don't want to embarrass myself."

"Uh... are we really back to that again?"

"Fine. Don't turn around, but this isn't going to work."

"I'll turn around." I did. "But try. Okay? It's worth the effort."

What she didn't get was I could get a much better sense of what was going on by feeling than seeing. Turning around wouldn't stop me from knowing exactly what was going on. And something was going on. She was getting closer. And then it stopped.

"You okay?" I forced myself not to face her.

"I thought I felt something."

"You did." Something big.

"How would you know?"

"I have my ways." I tried to bite back my smile before I turned back around.

"You are different than I thought."

"What did you think?" This I had to hear.

"I don't know. But not like this. This is different."

"Good different? Bad different?" I really hoped this wasn't bad different.

"Good." She pursed her lips. "I think."

"You want to try again?"

"Not really."

I laughed. Her honesty was refreshing. "Well, what else are you going to do?"

"I'm not sure. Evidently, I don't have another job unless Jonathan needs a break."

"Want to see if he needs a break?" I assumed Jonathan was the guy at the desk. I didn't want her to give up after one try, but I also didn't want to push her if she wasn't interested in being pushed. That wasn't going to end well.

"Now that sounds like a good idea. Besides, we really need to talk about how we are going to take on the rules."

"So now we are taking them on? Not changing them?"

She smiled. "Isn't that the same thing?"

"Taking them on sounds even more badass."

"What is with you wanting me to be badass?"

"It's not about want. I'm merely speaking the truth."

"What about you?" She swung her arms at her sides. "Are you badass?"

"Not like you are." I laughed.

"Oh, yes, you are. I mean you came here to find me." She smiled, and I felt it everywhere.

"I don't think that's badass. Desperate maybe."

"Nah. I don't think it's desperate. I don't get why you've waited so long to talk to me though."

"You seemed preoccupied, and you can be really intimidating."

"Me?" She put a hand to her chest. "How can I be intimidating?"

"You don't care what anyone thinks."

She snorted. I did a double take. It was actually kind of cute coming from her, but it was still surprising.

She put a hand to her face. "So, there you go. I care."

"But you don't act like you do."

"Maybe I'm just a good actor. I mean did you even know how embarrassed I was?"

"Not until you said something. But I don't actually think you were embarrassed."

"Yes, because you know how I feel better than I do."

"I never said that." I pushed open the door to the store and held it to let her step out.

"Hey, guys," Jonathan called from the desk. "What's up?"

"You want to take a break?" Glow offered.

"Sure." He got up from his perch behind the counter. "Thanks. I'm used to being the only one here."

"So how do you usually take breaks?"

"I just run to pee and stuff. I don't take breaks."

"You can tonight. I mean, Mr. Wayes never trained me or anything, but I figure I'll work it out."

"I highly doubt anyone will even come in. I'll be back in five, and I'll show you how to use the register and stuff."

"Cool." Glow eyed the register until Jonathan disappeared into the back. Then, she turned to me. "You can head home if you want."

"Trying to get rid of me?"

"No. But I have to be here. You don't."

"Don't think you're getting out of trying the magic again."

"Going to be my enforcer now?"

"I prefer to think of my role in this is as your coach and friend."

"Okay, coach and friend. Want a snack?"

"What are you thinking?"

"Chocolate." Her eyes lit up.

I laughed. "I am down with that. But how about we make that ice cream?"

"I like the way you think."

I walked over to the ice cream case and debated before grabbing the rocky road. "You like nuts in your ice cream?"

"What don't I like nuts in?" She winked.

I laughed once I accepted it was a joke. "Okay, then." I handed it to her. "Do you think we have to wait for Jonathan to ring it up?" I pulled a five out of my wallet. "At least take this so it doesn't look like we are stealing the merchandise."

"I should be paying for half."

"You can buy the next pint."

"Or I can get us a pint of beer another night. You know at Last Call." She seemed to be struggling to look at me as she spoke.

"Sounds great." I tried not to be surprised by her forwardness. A joke about nuts and an offer to buy me a beer. Was that her way of asking me out? Maybe Keegan was right. I was a chicken.

# GLOW

"*I* kind of asked him out." I did my best to play it cool as I relayed the events from the night before to Penny.

It was after 6 a.m. when I'd given up on Mr. Wayes coming back and returned to the dorm.

"What do you mean by kind of?" She paused from applying her makeup.

"He bought us a pint of ice cream to share. I offered to buy him a pint of beer at Last Call sometime."

"You did ask him out." She pointed at me. "There's no kind of about it."

"But I didn't give a specific day or anything. It was more of a general offer."

"Doesn't matter. You can ask someone out without getting into the specifics."

"Okay. Well, I did." And it felt both good and terrifying.

"That's awesome." Penny bounced in her chair. "I didn't even know you were into Lionel."

"I didn't know either."

"Wait. What?" She dropped her lipstick. "Then what made you ask him out?"

"I mean I already found him attractive, but it was more of a surface thing. Then he came by and I got to know him better. He's really cool."

"I love that about you." She picked up the fallen lipstick and applied it to her lips. Bright red. I could have never pulled off that color.

"Love what?"

"That you can make a decision like that. You liked hanging out with him for a few hours, so you asked him out. No debate. Nothing."

"If I'd needed to debate it, it wouldn't have been worth doing."

"I am envious of your decisiveness. And that you have a date with him. He's swoon worthy." She put her hands to her chest.

"What makes him swoon worthy?"

"Says the girl who asked him out?" Penny laughed.

"I think he's attractive. Very. And I have some other reasons. I was wondering yours."

"You go first." She zipped up her makeup bag. "After all, you are the one who's going to go out with him."

"It's a promise of a beer. Not exactly anything serious."

"All relationships have to start somewhere."

"He's trying to help me."

"Yeah?" Penny crossed one leg over the other. "That's pretty great of him."

"But I don't get why."

"Well, he accepted a date with you. Shouldn't that kind of tell you why? Or potentially why at least?"

"Wanting to grab a beer with me doesn't explain wanting to put time into helping me with magic. And he seems to really care."

"Is this part of why you like him?" Penny leaned forward in her chair. "That he seems to care about you?"

"It's part of it, obviously, but not everything. Yet, I can't help but worry there's some ulterior motive I'm missing here."

"There's always an ulterior motive. Always."

"That's a bit of a depressing way to view life." And surprising coming from her.

"I don't do depressing. You know that."

"So, that sounds depressing. Just so you know." Might as well call a spade a spade.

Penny tied her hair up in a perfectly done high pony-tail. "I don't see an ulterior motive here. At least not one that's worth dwelling on. If he helps you with your magic, you get to stay in Wolf Bound. We get to stay roommates. You get to have the life you've always dreamed of."

"I like how you put the roommate thing before the life I dreamed of."

"Priorities. Have to have the right priorities." She winked.

"Whatever you say, Penn."

"What did Mr. Wayes say about Lionel being there?"

"I don't think he knows. He never came back." And I didn't know if that was normal or not.

She read my mind. "That's kind of weird."

"Maybe, maybe not. Jonathan said he usually closes up himself."

"Are you going again tonight?"

"I think I have to." And I wanted to. Last night was the closest I'd gotten to actually reaching magic.

"Is Lionel coming to see you?" Penny made a kissy face.

"I wouldn't know."

"You didn't discuss it?"

"No."

"So you had time to set up a date, but not to discuss your next magic session?"

"We didn't set up a date. Remember? We only discussed the possibility of me buying us beers."

"Fine. Say what you want to say. But there's no denying a date is happening."

"Unless it doesn't. I may not see him again." And that disappointed me more than I wanted to admit.

"You'll see him. You guys have class together. Today actually."

She was right. "We do. Oh my gosh, I'm going to fall asleep."

"Not if I have anything to say about it." She got a twinkle in her eye.

"What are you going to do, Penny?"

"Nothing." She grinned before pulling one of her breakfast shakes out of the fridge. "Drink this."

"You know I hate those things." I wrinkled my nose. "Artificial vanilla is not my thing."

"It's more than a normal drink. Or you can choose to fall asleep in your classes and get in trouble. Is that what you want? More attention on you?"

I groaned. "Really...?"

"Come on." Penny handed me the shake.

I twisted the lid and took a sip. I tasted the magic immediately. "Couldn't you have hidden that taste?"

"You can taste it?" She took the drink and sipped it. "Tastes normal to me. Maybe you forgot what these drinks taste like."

I shrugged. "Maybe." I thought over what Lionel had said about me being particularly sensitive. It still seemed hard to believe I'd be able to taste magic Penny couldn't. Penny could do pretty much anything.

I wasn't all that excited to drink something magical, but if it kept me awake and out of trouble, I would try it.

"Feel any better?" Penny watched as I sipped it.

"Much. Thanks."

"Ready to go see Lionel?" she teased.

"I'm not going to see Lionel. I'm going to class."

"Correction. We are going to class." Penny pulled her own shake out of the fridge. "And I know what I'll be watching."

"Don't make things awkward." I wasn't going to do well with that.

"Who me?" She put a hand to her chest. "Would I ever do that?"

"Yes." I swung my tote bag over my shoulder. "Yes, you would."

"Well, I won't this time." She slipped her laptop into her bag and zipped it up. "I promise."

"I'm holding you to that." I opened the door, knowing she'd follow.

I tried not to stare at the door to the boys' hall as we headed toward the stairs, but Penny caught me. "I wonder what has your attention? Hoping to see someone?"

I gently bumped my shoulder into hers. "Geez, Penny. Way to be discreet."

"Come on, there's no one around." We started down the stairs.

I FORCED myself to stay focused straight ahead on our walk over to potions. I wasn't going to give Penny any more ammo than she already had. She meant well, but boy could that girl tease.

We reached the magic arts building and headed inside to our classroom. Most of the class was already seated. But not Lionel. I was sure that wasn't lost on Penny either.

"Hopefully, he made himself a breakfast elixir too," Penny whispered as we settled into our seats.

He couldn't, but I couldn't tell her that. "He didn't stay with me the whole time last night. I made him leave."

"Made him, huh?" Penny opened her laptop to get herself ready. We were seated at one of a dozen large black lab tables on tall stools that were anything but comfortable.

I opened to a fresh page in my notebook. A quick glance around the room reminded me that I was the only one not seated behind a computer screen.

I glanced at the clock on the wall. Class started in three minutes. Hopefully, Lionel made it. Like me, he was skating on thin ice with the school.

Professor Cummings walked in, and Lionel slipped into his spot next to Keeton just in time. He sat one row back on the other side of the room. I glanced over and caught his eye. He smiled before returning his attention to setting up his laptop.

"Good morning, class," Professor Cummings started in a completely monotone voice. I was feeling extra grateful for the magic Penny had used for me. It wouldn't have taken me long to fall asleep otherwise.

"Good morning!" Without meaning to, I replied with way more zest than normal. Boy, that drink worked. It also got me some funny stares. Lionel quirked an eyebrow.

"Then, let's get started. Shall we?" Professor Cummings's monotone never changed.

I bit my tongue to stop myself from saying anything in agreement.

"We'll continue our study of charm spells today. From the reading, which I am sure you all have done, you already know that, although these spells are relatively easy to cast, they do come with sizable risk."

Penny raised her hand.

Professor Cummings nodded at her. "Yes, Ms. Tanger."

"Don't all spells have risks?"

"Yes. But note I said sizable."

"True... but is it really worse than any other?"

"Yes." The professor nodded. "Because a charm spell is designed to influence the feelings an individual has for another. This may have a significant impact on the behavior and choices of the affected party. Even lifelong impacts."

"You mean if you charm a girl and get her pregnant," Carlton called out.

Penny glared at him. "Figures you'd say that."

"That is one potential consequence, but there are others. Countless others."

I raised my hand. "Are there rules in place to control the use of charms?"

Carlton laughed. "Why bother asking, Glow? You'll never be able to cast one."

"Shut up, Carlton," Lionel snapped. "You're the one who'll need a charm to ever get laid."

I smiled. I didn't need someone to defend me, but I also didn't mind. I appreciated that he was willing to do it.

"All right. That's enough of that." Mr. Cummings frowned. "My point in all of this is to remind you that just because a form of magic is easy, doesn't mean it should be used lightly. No form of magic should be used lightly."

"Of course not." Penny folded her hands in front of her. "That's a pretty basic concept."

"It is, Ms. Tanger, but not everyone in this room understands that. That is pretty obvious from the responses I got."

"Who would like to practice a charm in front of the class?" the professor asked. "Who wants to go first?"

I slumped in my seat. This was always the worst part. I couldn't. Or rather, I couldn't be the one to use the magic; I could always be the one who the magic was used on.

Penny raised her hand as she always did, and the professor ignored her. He looked at Lionel who did not have his hand raised. "What about you, Mr. Daniels? You up for the challenge?"

"Sure." Lionel stood up and walked to the front of the room.

I watched him, wishing I didn't immediately notice how good the light stubble on his face looked. Or that I didn't have the urge to run my hands through his hair. But I did, and there was absolutely nothing I could do about it.

"I'm going to do an attachment charm," Lionel announced.

"Very well." The professor settled back into his chair behind the front table. "Carry on."

Lionel winked at me before turning his attention to Carlton, who was busy whispering something to the guy sitting next to him.

Then suddenly, Carlton picked up his textbook and hugged it. "Mine."

The class laughed.

"Mine. Mine!" Carlton held the book against his chest. "Mine!"

There was more laughing.

Professor Cummings smiled for a brief moment before his face turned serious again. "Now, please do the equally important part—remove the charm."

"Yes, sir." Lionel looked back at Carlton, who slowly lowered the book to the table.

Carlton blinked a few times before looking down at the book. "What happened?"

"You don't remember?" the professor asked.

"I seemed to really care about my book." He picked up the book as if trying to understand the appeal.

"Mr. Daniels used an attachment spell on you. It appeared to be very effective," the professor explained.

Carlton glared at Lionel.

Lionel shrugged before returning to his seat.

"Thank you for the demonstration, Mr. Daniels. And based on Mr. Page's reaction, I see it helped prove my point. Even something as seemingly innocuous as a charm spell to create an attachment to an inanimate object caused confusion. Imagine what would have happened if Lionel had chosen a living target for attachment. I am grateful he so wisely chose not to."

The professor was right. It had been a wise choice. Lionel didn't need any more enemies, although by the looks of it, Carlton was plenty angry over the book.

"I trust most of you can handle a simple attachment spell like that." Professor Cummings's eyes darted over to me and then away. I tried to ignore the stomach-sinking feeling. "But, do you know what to do if you can't release an attachment spell? What if Mr. Daniels had lost control of the charm? What could he have done?"

Penny raised her hand.

"Yes, Ms. Tanger."

"He didn't lose control, now did he? If you can't keep control of a charm, you shouldn't be using it in the first place."

"That is what we all aim for, but sometimes, no matter how well we prepare, we lose control."

"He could have woven another charm. He could have sought help from a peer or a teacher." Penny didn't wait to be called on again before starting in on the suggestions.

I raised my hand. The professor called on me. Even if I couldn't use magic, that didn't mean I didn't study hard and know a lot about it. "He could have calmed down, changed positions, and tried again to release it."

I gave Lionel a tiny glance and found him grinning. I figured he wouldn't mind me using his advice.

"Very smart advice, Ms. Mayer." Professor Cummings stood up. "Sometimes, all it takes is a small change in position to stay in control."

The rest of class went quickly, and before I knew it, Penny and I were packing up and heading out of the room.

"That was a really great idea," Lionel whispered from

behind me. "The whole change position thing. I wonder where you came up with it."

"I don't know. Some guy told me." I slowed down a little so we were walking side by side.

Penny looked between us. "Wow. Already have inside jokes? That's so cute."

"It's not an inside joke." I bristled.

"Well, it kind of is," Lionel contradicted.

"I heard you really helped my girl here." Penny put her hand over my shoulder. "That's cool of you."

"I didn't do much. She has everything she needs. She just needs to push herself a bit more."

"Well, she came home this morning in a very good mood."

"I wish she were coming home in a good mood from something else." He nudged my shoulder with his.

I felt the blood rushing to my face. Now that was unexpected.

"Sorry. I couldn't help it. It's like your nuts comment..."

"Nuts comment?" Penny's brow furrowed. "Is that another inside joke?"

"No," I said, just as he said, "Yes."

"You two should at least get on the same page." Penny pursed her lips, then it turned into a smile. "But I had better run. Have fun." She winked and hurried off.

"What kind of fun does she expect us to have?" Lionel asked.

"Who knows?" I knew exactly what she meant, but I

wasn't going to say anything. "But I won't complain. She kind of saved me today."

"She did a wakeup spell for you, huh?"

"That obvious?"

"Your response to the professor was a bit over-the-top, not to mention you should be exhausted if you really didn't get in until this morning."

"You were up pretty late too," I pointed out.

"Not as late as you. Not that I would have left if you hadn't made me."

"You were yawning. I wasn't going to make you stay." I was the one who needed the work time, not him.

"Okay. In the future I won't yawn."

"Good." Him not needing to be there didn't mean I didn't want him there.

"Do you have another class now?" he asked.

"Yeah. Math. I'm loading up on some basic courses. You know, as I'll probably be transferring to a regular college next year."

"No. You won't be. I'm not going to let that happen. Remember?"

"Well, I didn't know that before I registered." And I still wasn't convinced we could pull this off in time. It was better to play it safe than be sorry. Although no matter how prepared I was course wise, I would never be prepared for the disappointment.

"True. I suppose you didn't. But math? What kind?"

"Statistics. The really fun stuff."

"Oh, yes. Thrilling."

"Do you have class now?" I hadn't asked before we started walking across the quad.

"Just Moon Phases. I didn't take it last semester."

"If you need my notes, let me know."

"Cool. Thanks."

We reached the general academics building. "Well, this is my stop."

"Want to meet for dinner around six? We can strategize for tonight?"

"Uh, sure." I tried to downplay my reaction, but I was glad he was the one who asked. "Sounds great."

"Okay. Don't have too much fun in stats." He grinned before walking back across the quad. I realized he'd traveled far out of his way to walk me to class.

Kind of like when he jumped to my defense. I didn't want to like it, but I did.

I allowed myself to enjoy the feeling as I made my way into stats class. At least I didn't lack the ability to succeed at this one.

## LIONEL

*I* couldn't ignore the phone calls much longer. I already had three voicemails, and I knew each call cost him a lot. Eventually, I'd have to return the call and do my duty. My duty as a son that is.

I had some time before I was due to meet Glow for dinner and my roommate, Terrance, was out until at least then. I had absolutely no excuse. It was time to call him back.

My call went to the connection desk at the Almandy Shifter Prison.

"Almandy Prison. How may I direct your call?"

"My name is Lionel Daniels. I would like to speak to Mathias Pillar, please."

"What is the nature of your communication?"

"Returning a call."

"And do you have a relationship with this prisoner?"

"Yes, I'm his son." It still made my stomach roll to

acknowledge that connection, but I didn't have much other choice.

I waited on the line before she connected me.

"Hello, son." His voice was hoarse and largely unfamiliar.

Son? The man had never called me that before. "Hello, Mathias."

"Is that anyway for you to address your father?"

"I haven't seen you enough to know how to address you any other way."

"Communication goes both ways, boy."

Boy? Because son wasn't bad enough. "I got your messages. What do you want?" If he expected a warm response from me, he had another thing coming.

"Watch yourself, Lionel."

Now he used my name.

"Your messages only told me to call. Not what do you want to talk about?" I fought the urge to hang up. My anger was rising, and I was running out of patience.

"I need to speak with you in person. You need to come down here."

"Down there? To the prison? You expect me to come down to the prison?"

"Yes. I need you. It's urgent."

"And what if I don't?" I wasn't going to let him push me around.

"You know the outcome of this trial is important to all of us. Even your mother."

And he'd done it. He hit my weakness. I'd protect my

mother no matter the cost. "I'll see how soon I can get there."

"Don't wait too long."

"I won't." I hung up. What had I just agreed to?"

* * *

"HE WANTS YOU TO GO THERE?" Glow set down her spoon beside her empty bowl of soup. "Wow. That's pretty big. Right? I mean from a man you barely know."

"Exactly. And normally I'd have told him to shove it, but I couldn't. He's right. If things go wrong, my mom is going to be pulled in."

"I'll go with you." She put her hands in front of her on the table. "Just tell me when, and I'll be ready to go."

"You will?" Was Glow seriously offering to drive four hours with me to go to Almandy Prison? Either she was crazy, or she wanted to be supportive. I assumed it was a little bit of both.

"Yes. I will." She nodded.

"Why? I mean I appreciate you offering. But why are you willing to? You know what kind of place it is." I didn't want her there even if the sound of her company sounded good. I didn't want to put her into any sort of bad situation.

"It's a long drive. We can plan together. Plus, I figure it might be easier for you if you're not alone. I could wait in the car though. If you'd prefer."

"I'd love the company, but you don't have to come."

"I know I don't have to, but I will. Okay?"

"Okay." I didn't want to even bring up my safety concerns out of fear of insulting her. Not to mention I wanted her company. "Sounds good. I probably can't wait too long."

"I'll go whenever."

"This weekend?" It was already Wednesday, so that didn't leave much time, but my father had made it sound pretty urgent.

"Sure." She sipped her water.

"Okay. That gives us a couple more nights to work on your magic." I was determined to see how much further we could push it.

"Mr. Wayes may stick around tonight." She swirled her straw around her glass.

"He may." I hadn't seen him at all the night before, but I assumed I would eventually. "Does that change anything?"

"No, I suppose not."

"Good." At least she wasn't trying to hide we were working together. "Okay if I come around about the same time again?"

"Sure. That sounds good. And I'm sorry."

"Sorry?" Her apology caught me off guard. "Why are you sorry?"

"That you have to deal with all of this with your dad."

"We both have a lot to deal with." Neither of us was currently living the easy life.

"We do." What I didn't say out loud was it was probably going to be far better if we had each other.

"Is this a private dinner?" Keeton walked over with Penny. The two of them didn't often hang out, so I assumed they'd probably been talking about us. There were worse things.

"Of course not." Glow pulled out the chair next to her.

"Okay. Just checking." Penny took a seat.

I shot Keeton a knowing look. I hoped he didn't say something stupid.

"Why are you looking at me that way?" Keeton sat down beside Penny, leaving me facing all three of them.

"Don't worry about it." Sometimes Keeton was so oblivious.

"We're discussing how to best deal with the crap that comes your way in life." Glow picked up a french fry from her tray. "Either of you have any thoughts on the subject?"

"That's easy." Keeton poured ketchup on his burger. "You say screw it."

"Oh?" Penny placed a napkin on her lap. "That fixes everything?"

"Not everything. But a lot. A whole lot."

"I try to work through my problems." Penny carefully placed her straw between her lips in a way that seemed intended to avoid ruining her lipstick. "It generally works."

"Agreed. But generally isn't always." Glow dipped a fry in ketchup.

"You're trying to work through your problem now and it's working." Penny took another one of her awkward sips. "It's working even better than you expected."

I knew exactly what she meant. "True, but I haven't solved it yet. And we aren't only talking about my issue."

"And you'll be fine too, Lionel." Keeton polished off his burger. The kid could eat.

"Why wouldn't Lionel be okay?" Penny looked at me funny. I was sure she was shocked there was something going on she wasn't in the know about.

"Nothing." Keeton mouthed an apology. "I was just being stupid."

"Nuh-uh." Penny shook her head. "You were not."

"It's nothing exciting." I decided to just spill it. "My father is on trial, and I have a block put on my magic use. No biggie."

"Wait. What?" Penny leaned forward on her elbow. "How isn't that a big deal? That's not fair. You are just going to sit back and take it?"

"I would rather not get expelled or arrested or worse." It's not like Penny would have done anything different.

"True." Penny removed her elbow from the table. "But that doesn't mean I can't find a way to help."

"Please don't." Great. This was all I needed. "It's not that I don't appreciate your concern, but I want to keep this quiet while I figure things out."

"If you say so. But you're not alone. The house will stand by you."

"Well, some of the house." Keeton chuckled. "You really pissed Carlton off today."

l shrugged. "So worth it."

"It was pretty awesome." Keeton reached over and took one of the few remaining fries on my plate. "But you should have faked not being able to end the charm."

"That would have been getting myself in trouble..."

"Oh, yes. You can't have fun this semester." Keeton dug into his slice of chocolate cake.

"I can have fun..." I glanced in Glow's direction. She blushed. Damn, I loved that blush. Everything about her was hot.

"You going to get your homework done before you go to work?" Penny took a bite of her chicken sandwich.

Glow set down her empty cup. "You're worried about me?"

"Well, it would be quite a shame if you get the magic going but still get kicked out because you fail other stuff." Penny ripped off a piece of lettuce sticking a little bit off the bun.

"True. I'll try to avoid that." Glow smiled as though she were thinking of something funny. I wished I knew what it was.

"Can't you do some of that at work?" Keeton asked. "I can't imagine Convenience is that busy all night."

"She's working on magic there," Penny explained.

"The whole time?" Keeton slumped in his chair.

When Glow didn't answer, I jumped in. "Mostly. We also took an ice cream break last night."

"Geez, Lionel, way to out us." Glow smiled.

"Okay." Keeton looked between us. "Is ice cream a euphemism for sex or something?"

"Hell no." Penny dropped her fork, and it made a

loud clanking sound when it hit the plate. "Not that sex would be bad, but her not telling me would be."

"Ice cream is not a euphemism for sex. We had ice cream." Glow frowned.

She was uncomfortable, which meant we really needed to move away from this conversation.

"If you say so." Keeton expression said it all. He didn't believe us.

"And on that note." Glow pushed back her chair. "Maybe I should go do that homework."

"Aww, come on." Keeton straightened in his seat. "I'm just messing with you guys. Learn to take a little teasing."

"I can take plenty of teasing. But as Penny said, I don't want to fail." Her voice was harsher than normal.

"Come on, dish it back." Keeton leaned forward on both elbows. "You'll feel better."

"Okay. Want me to?" Glow crossed her arms.

I watched anxiously.

"You only wish you had someone to have ice cream with."

Keeton laughed. "Ice cream or *ice cream*."

"Either."

"Keeton can find plenty of girls to have ice cream with." Penny raised her chin.

"Which kind of ice cream?" I had to ask. And what was with Penny coming to Keeton's defense. Was there something going on with them?

But it didn't matter; Glow still looked incredibly

uncomfortable. "All right, Glow, you want to head to the library for a bit before work?"

"Sure. I just need to grab some stuff from my room." She pushed her chair back. "See you guys later."

Penny smiled. "I hope work goes well."

"Same here." Keeton gave a wave. "And sorry if I pissed you off, but you walked right into it."

Once we made it outside, I decided to do some damage control. "Sorry about him." Keeton was a good friend, but he could also be pretty annoying sometimes.

"Don't be. Penny was doing her worst too. I was fine, just starting to get stressed again. That's all."

"Penny has her moments. That's for sure."

"But she means well. Plus, she's the only one who's stayed by my side through all this." Glow glanced back toward the dining hall.

"I'm sorry I wasn't supportive before this. It wasn't that I didn't care. I just didn't think you wanted anyone around. You seemed a bit standoffish."

"Sometimes, it's easier to block people out rather than deal with ridicule." She picked up her pace as we neared the Wolf Bound dorm.

"I'd never ridicule you. Maybe some teasing, but that's it."

She stopped. "What's with you guys and teasing?"

"Teasing just makes things more fun sometimes."

"If you say so." She looked away, but I noticed a little smile.

Fifteen minutes later, we were headed to the library.

"Hey." A guy waved at Glow as we crossed the mostly empty quad.

"Hey." Glow held up a hand in greeting.

"I haven't seen you around much. You doing okay?" the guy asked.

"Uh... yeah. I'm fine." Glow gave me a look I didn't immediately understand before continuing across the quad. Once we were out of earshot from the kid, she leaned in. "Do you know who that was?"

"SHOULD I?" It wasn't a giant school, so I knew most of the students, but I didn't know that kid's name or anything.

"I've seen him around, but we've never talked."

"It sure seemed like he knew you, but maybe he just thought you were cute. I can't say I'd blame him."

She swatted at my arm. "Be serious. That was weird."

"Maybe he had you confused with someone else," I suggested.

"Maybe." She didn't sound convinced.

"We can turn around and talk to him."

"No." She shook her head. "Let's get to the library. It's going to be time for work before I know it."

"Okay. If you're sure." I glanced back and could just make out the back of the guy. Hopefully, we didn't have any other weird run-ins. Glow needed to stay focused if she was going to pull out her magic.

Thankfully, the rest of the walk to the library was uneventful, and we set up at my usual table in the stacks. I hadn't given much thought to it until we were both seated in a quiet spot along the back wall.

"Do you study here a lot?" she asked.

"Define a lot." I didn't live at the library, but I liked to study somewhere other than my room when given the option.

"Ever?"

"Yes, I'm here a few times a week."

"I am too. Weird I've never seen you."

"I've seen you." I let the words slip out without considering what I was saying. "Not that I was watching you or anything."

She raised an eyebrow. "Any reason you never said hello? And no blaming it on being 'standoffish'." She made air quotes when she said standoffish.

"I was nervous I guess." And I sounded lame and obsessed.

"I can't imagine you'd ever be nervous because of me."

"Is that so? You've never liked someone so much you were nervous about getting shot down?" I had already embarrassed myself. There was no reason to stop now.

"You liked me that much?"

"Yeah, I did."

"But you've dated other girls... I've seen you."

"But those girls weren't you. Way less intimidating." And there was way less to lose.

"There is nothing intimidating about me."

"You have this confidence to you. I envy it really."

"Seriously?" She opened her notebook to a page full of handwritten notes. She was the only student I knew who still took her class notes by hand.

"Yeah. It's amazing."

"You have the same confidence. Other than with me evidently." She smiled.

"We need to get that beer you promised me. When can I take you up on it?"

"Do we need a set time?" She hooked her pen in the spiral of her notebook.

"Yes. That way it happens."

"Isn't a road trip more of a promise than a beer?"

"We're not counting a road trip to a prison as our first date."

"First date?" She looked at me.

"Yeah. The beer offer was for a date, right?" I had admitted so much already. No reason to backpedal.

"Right. Well, how about tomorrow night?"

"Sounds perfect." And soon. I was definitely done with waiting.

"But right now, we should study." She tapped her notebook.

"Absolutely." I knew there was no way I'd be able to concentrate, but I'd do my best to stay quiet while letting her know I couldn't take my eyes off her.

# GLOW

*H*e was late, but I wouldn't read into it. People were late all the time. There were tons of reasons, most of them completely acceptable. I'd never realized how quickly I jumped to rationalize things, but evidently, I did.

"Can I get you anything?" a female bartender with dark brown hair just a touch longer than shoulder length asked. It was the second time she'd come over, and thankfully, she hadn't told me to get lost yet.

Still, I didn't really want to sit there without something to drink much longer. "Uh, that local wheat beer you just started carrying. Thanks." I didn't actually plan to drink more than one beer, but I figured I'd look less awkward if I had something in my hands.

My phone buzzed, and I pulled it out.

**So sorry. I'll explain when I see you. On my way.**

The bartender set the bottle of beer down in front of me, and I took a sip. I'd been right not to worry. He wasn't standing me up.

"Long day?" Ryan, a Wolf Born guy I'd had a few classes with first semester, sat down next to me.

I took another sip of beer. "Not too bad."

"Then why so glum?" He ordered an IPA.

"Just waiting for someone."

"A guy someone?" He leaned back on his elbows.

"Maybe."

He laughed. "By the way, how's the uh, magic coming?"

I held in a groan. "You know about that?"

"I do... and I actually think I might be able to help."

Now he had my attention. "How?" I tried not to get my hopes up. I was already walking a dangerous line.

"You know my girlfriend, right? Nadia?"

"Yeah. I've met her." She'd seemed nice enough, if a bit shy.

"She's really smart, and if anyone can find answers, it's her." He sipped his beer.

"Well, I'll try anything. I'm running out of time."

"And if they don't come, I'll see what I can do in Wolf Born. I can't promise anything though." He looked at his beer rather than at me.

"I totally get it." He didn't need to explain himself. "I know how this works."

Ryan seemed like the type that would be an arrogant asshole, but he most definitely wasn't. Nadia was lucky. He was as nice as he was easy on the eyes.

He glanced at his watch. "Well, I have to head out, or I'll keep Nadia waiting." He downed the rest of his beer before setting it on the bar. "I hope this maybe a guy person shows up soon." Ryan walked out the front door.

A few minutes later, Lionel ran inside, out of breath. He was known for being a great runner even in human form. If he was out of breath, he must have really been sprinting. "Please don't hate me."

"Hate you?" Was he kidding?

"For leaving you waiting by yourself for so long. I'm really sorry about that."

"It wasn't that long."

"Thirty-five minutes is long by most standards." He took a seat on the stool Ryan had just vacated.

"Well, not my standard."

He smiled. "Have I told you lately how awesome you are?"

"Not until just now." I turned on my stool, so my body faced his. "But what would make you awesome is if you told me why you were late." No reason to beat around the bush.

He pushed up the sleeves of his shirt. "I was getting my official notice from the academy."

"Official notice?" That didn't sound good.

"Let me get a beer first. I need it."

"Wait. It's my treat, remember?" I got the bartender's attention and ordered a beer for him.

I waited until he'd taken a big sip, hoping he'd explain more.

He set the bottle down. "My official notice telling me

that if I found a work around to remove the block myself I'm expelled."

"That is still so crazy."

"That is no crazier than telling a wolf so full of magic that if she can't wield it by some artificial date she's out. We've already been over this."

"We have." I sipped my beer. "But I'm no closer to finding a solution."

"We are going to need to buy in from bigger players."

"Bigger players?"

"Yeah. From different houses. Speaking of, I saw Ryan Grayson on my way over."

"I was just talking to him. He suggested I talk to his girlfriend, Nadia, about my issue."

"Can't hurt. And if we get him on our side..." He rolled his shoulders back as if trying to relieve tension. I had an urge to help him with it, to give him a back rub.

"You don't have to tell me." As someone who was actively looking into a transfer to Wolf Born, I knew all about the big families and the pull they had at the academy.

"You really want to do this road trip with me?" He paused with his beer midway to his lips.

"Of course."

"Of course?" He raised an eyebrow. "There's not much of course about it."

"Sure there is. I said I was coming. What would make me change my mind?"

"A reality check." He scooted his stool a little bit

closer to mine. "This isn't a small thing for you to agree to."

"Yeah, well having you help me with my problem isn't small either. By the way, you can't get in trouble, right? By helping me?"

"I'm not using my magic, so I don't see why anyone would have a problem at all."

"If they thought you were..." If there was even a chance of that happening, we had to stop.

"But I'm not. So we are fine."

I wanted to believe him because I wanted his help. "What time were you coming by tonight?"

"When do you want me to come by?" He turned the question on me.

"Eleven? That work for you?"

"Absolutely. And I also think it's badass you are having a beer before work."

"Badass or irresponsible? There is a very fine line."

"Can't hurt with the real reason you are there. You know, it could loosen you up or something."

"Still seems irresponsible to drink before work."

"Well, not much you can do about it now." He tapped his beer bottle against mine. "Just keep it to one."

"I'll be done with this one soon."

"Then two. Just keep it to two."

I laughed. "I can switch to water after this."

"You could, or you couldn't. You aren't irresponsible either way."

"You just want me to have another beer."

"And why would I want that?" He rested his hand right next to mine.

"Because you are always right, and you seem to think drinking will relax me."

"I thought you were going to say I wanted to see you drunk."

"Well, there is that too, but it's going to take a whole lot more than two beers to get me there."

"Got some real tolerance, huh?" He moved, and his hand brushed against mine. Even that small touch sent a wave of awareness through me.

"Yeah. Not sure if that's a good thing."

"It's a bad thing for your wallet and liver, but a good thing otherwise."

"You're funny."

"I am?" He hooked his fingers around mine.

I made no effort to move my hand. His hand was warm and comfortable, yet it also hinted at so much more. "Yeah."

"Any particular reason why I am?"

"No." I shook my head. "You just are."

"Well, cheers to that." He held up his bottle, and I tapped mine against his. Maybe he was right. A second beer couldn't hurt.

"You've been drinking, haven't you?" Mr. Wayes greeted me as soon as I entered the back room of Convenience.

Whoa, that was fast. "Yes. I'm sorry. I probably shouldn't have been, but I was grabbing a drink with Lionel and we talked about how it might help." Maybe I should have left Lionel out of it, but it kind of slipped out.

Mr. Wayes smiled. "Ah, you were with Lionel again?"

"Yes." Again? So, he knew he'd been around the night before? "And it isn't his fault, but we were discussing ways to make this process easier."

"And the idea isn't a bad one. Alcohol loosens inhibitions, and loosening inhibitions can help with releasing latent abilities."

"So you aren't mad?" I really hoped I hadn't screwed things up.

"No. Why would I be mad? You are here to help yourself. Figure all that out, and I'll find more work for you."

"Telling me you'll have more work for me isn't exactly an inducement to figure things out."

"You have plenty of reasons to figure things out. I don't have to give you any more," he pointed out.

"True enough."

"But I do need to ask you one thing." Mr. Wayes walked down an aisle, tapping box after box.

"Yes?"

"How did Lionel get involved?"

"I don't know." I thought over how the night had gone. "He just showed up."

"He's interested in you." There was no question in his words.

"Yes." I knew that, and I wasn't going to deny it. "And I think I'm interested in him."

"You think?" Mr. Wayes raised an eyebrow.

"I mean, I'm definitely interested, but I'm not sure if a relationship is the right thing for me right now. I may be leaving soon."

"You aren't leaving, but only you know whether a relationship is a good idea or not."

"Yeah, I figured you'd say that." Which was funny. How did I know what this man was going to say when I'd just met him?

"Here. I need to show you something." He led the way in the opposite direction from the restricted section.

"Where are we going?" I was going to follow him regardless of what he said, but that didn't mean I didn't want to be prepared.

"Why ask the question when you are going to find out momentarily?"

"Fine. I can be patient." I followed behind him, noting that it felt so much longer since the first time.

He pulled out a key and opened the door to a small room. He flipped on a light to illuminate what appeared to be an ordinary, windowless office, with a small desk in the corner and a single chair behind it. There were cabinets lining all of the other walls.

"You may find what you need in here."

"What do you mean?" I glanced around. "What am I missing?"

"I don't know? What are you missing?" He walked

right back out the way we'd come in, closing the door behind him, leaving me in the cramped space.

"Okay, then." I looked around again. It was hard to know if I was supposed to be searching for magic the way I'd done the night before, or instead physically searching the cabinets. It was impossible to know, and I was sure that was intentional.

It was up to me. First step: search for magic. I could almost hear Lionel's voice in my head.

I eyed the black swivel chair, but I discarded the idea. I was definitely more of a floor girl.

I settled on the floor and closed my eyes. And there it was—warmth. Magic everywhere.

I focused more. Nothing. I got up and turned off the lights. The room was pitch black, not even my strong night vision kicked in. I slid down to the floor right there and settled back in. Moving farther into the room seemed ill-advised, and knowing me, I'd stumble into a filing cabinet or something. I reached out again, and this time, it was there in all its blazing glory.

I opened my eyes, and without turning on the lights, headed to one of the cabinets. It glowed. I wasn't sure if it was really glowing, or if it was the knowledge of what was in there.

I opened the drawer and pulled out what looked to be a centuries-old book. It was falling apart, but the contents were still clear. It was full of spells. Each page was hand-written. A handwritten spell book? Those were nearly impossible to find anymore.

I flipped through the pages. This was crazy. I settled

back into my spot on the floor and started studying what I saw. I ran my fingers over the words, and I could feel it. I could feel energy reaching out to me. The warm feeling grew stronger and stronger, until it was almost uncomfortable. Almost because it was still a relief. I could have been burned, and I would have still been happy.

The door opened, and I reflectively closed the book.

"Sitting in the dark, are you?"

My shoulders relaxed at the sound of Lionel's voice. "It's not dark. I can read this."

"You found the glow!" He closed the door and sat down next to me. "This is incredible."

"I know." I opened the book again, eager to see what else I could find.

"And how did you find it?" His voice was full of excitement; I could tell he actually cared.

"I found a good spot in the dark."

He laughed. "Maybe the beer helped..."

"Or this room. Mr. Wayes hadn't brought me here before." And I was positive he'd brought me there for a reason. He'd known what I would find. At least, I assumed he did.

"I'm sure he had his reasons."

"Did he tell you I was here?" I wondered if they'd crossed paths this time.

"No. You are easy for me to find." He stretched out his legs in front of him.

"That's kind of crazy. I'm that easy to find through magic?" I wondered if he could find everyone that way.

"No. Not through magic. I can't use magic right now.

Remember?"

"How could I forget? I mean you can sense magic in me?"

"Yes, and now you know for sure you have it. You wielded it." There was something akin to awe in his voice.

"But that's not going to be enough to keep me at the academy. I'm supposed to be further advanced by now."

"But it's a great start. A really great start."

"True." Everyone had to start somewhere. And maybe showing some potential would be enough to get me through the semester.

"So what have you found in there so far?"

"All sorts of things. Have you ever heard of a guiding charm? You can actually set out an invisible magic path for someone to find. And by someone, I mean someone specific. It will be hidden from everyone else, magic or not." I could feel the excitement oozing out of me.

"I've heard of it, but I've never seen it written out." He leaned over to get a look at this page. "Look at this handwriting. It's beautiful. And really old."

"I know. Was Mr. Wayes up front when you came in? I need to know who wrote this."

"I didn't see him, but he could be back here somewhere. This back room is pretty much endless, you know."

"I know. That must be quite a hard spell to perfect. I've heard of expansion spells, but I feel like this place is unreal."

"It's a difficult spell, but also useful. Maybe it's in

here."

We took turns flipping through the book, and almost every page had something cool on it. We could have spent all night looking through it.

I yawned.

He started to close the book. "You need sleep."

I put my finger on the page to stop him from closing the cover completely. "I can get another elixir from Penny."

"No. You need sleep. I'm walking you back now."

"But Mr. Wayes." I moved my finger from the page, wanting to continue, but not really wanting to fight. I was exhausted.

"Mr. Wayes would say get sleep. It's not like you are actually running the store. That's Jonathan's job."

"Shouldn't he be tired?" If he could stay up all night, so could I.

"He's a grad student. He doesn't have morning classes. I've discussed this with him."

"When?" How had I missed that?

"When I showed up tonight."

"Thanks."

"For?"

"For showing up again."

"I want to be here, so I am." His arm brushed against mine.

"Yeah, but it's cool that you want to be here."

He put his hand over mine, and the touch sent something through me. "You should get used to me wanting to be with you."

"Yeah?" I looked deep into his eyes, looking for something. Some hint that his words weren't true. But I found nothing.

"And I want to be around you, which means you have to take care of yourself so I'm getting you back to your room to sleep."

"Lionel?" I loved the way his name felt when it slipped off my tongue.

"Yeah?" He turned toward me.

"Never mind."

"No. Tell me what you were going to say."

"It wasn't something I was going to say. Something I wanted to do."

"Yeah?" He leaned in.

"Yeah." I tried to build up the courage. Now that I opened the can of worms, I wasn't about to put the lid back on.

"Well, there's something I want to do too."

"Separate from getting me home to sleep?" I kept my eyes fixed on his. If I looked away, I was going to chicken out.

"Yeah."

"Then do it."

"Okay." His lips brushed against mine, light at first, but then harder. He bit down on my lip, and I knew I was gone. I moaned as he pushed into my mouth. I gladly gave him access and wrapped my arms around his neck.

The kiss continued, and I eventually found myself straddling his lap. I'd never crawled into a guy's lap in my life. Yet there I was, pressing my body against his in a dark room. Reality hit me, and I broke the kiss. I started to get off his lap, but he held me in place. "Where are you going?"

"I'm getting off your lap." I didn't really try to move again. I was comfortable in his arms.

"Any reason why?"

"Because I can't just sit on your lap."

"Why not?" He ran a hand through my hair.

"Because I shouldn't be."

"Yes, you should." He brushed his lips against mine. "Is that what you wanted to do as well?"

"Yes. That is exactly what I wanted to do." Although, I hadn't planned for things to get quite so hot or that I'd end up on his lap.

"Convenient we were on the same page."

"Very convenient." I looked at his lips. His unbelievably enticing lips.

"You know what else is convenient?"

"What?"

"That we live in the same dorm."

"On the same floor." That was both dangerous and convenient.

"We do..."

"But not tonight. We can't enjoy that tonight." No matter how nice a thought enjoying that convenience would be.

"You mean you don't think Penny would be happy if you brought me home?"

I laughed. "Oh, she'd be happy. But didn't we already discuss how much I needed to sleep?"

"We did..."

I pushed against his arms again, and this time he released me. I slid off his lap and picked up the book from where I'd placed it.

"Do you think I should leave this here or take it?"

"I'd take it. You found the book for a reason, and you need to figure out what else it can do for you."

"And for you... maybe there's something in there that can help us help you."

"Put a spell on the administration?" I suggested. "Okay. Not that extreme. But maybe open everyone up to making changes."

"I like the idea and sentiment, but I want to be careful with any magic I touch." He took my hand in his.

"I wasn't saying you had to touch the magic at all." I didn't want to get him in trouble or anything.

"It would be guilt by association... I mean we are associated now."

"And we may end up even more associated." I sure hoped we would.

"I sure hope we will." He read my mind.

I smiled. "Me too."

"All right, we should go before I end up kissing you again." He pressed his lips to my forehead.

"Like that's a bad thing."

"Is that your way of asking me to kiss you again?"

"Maybe..." I grinned.

"All right. It's really hard for me to say no to you." His arms wrapped around me, and the next thing I knew, I was back on his lap with his lips were back on mine.

## LIONEL

*H*ours later and I still tasted her. I tasted the sweetness of her lips, and that minty flavor buried deep inside her mouth. I lay in bed, trying to sleep, but unable to do anything but think of her.

She'd been so excited about the book, and that excitement had taken her already gorgeous face and added a glow to it.

I could not get her out of my head, and I knew there was no chance I was falling asleep.

"You okay, man?" My roommate, Terrance, sat up in bed.

"Yeah, why?" I hadn't said anything out loud.

"You know I can sense these types of things." He turned on his lamp, which was completely unnecessary.

I blinked a few times, trying to get used to the new light. "Yeah.. I guess I'd forgotten." I could sense magic. He could sense emotions. We were an interesting set of roommates.

"So what's going on? What has your emotions so crazed?"

"It's a good thing. I assure you." A very good thing. Even if I was unbelievably sexually frustrated.

"Oh yeah?" He laughed. "My mistake. This is a good thing. It's Glow, isn't it?"

"Who else?" Even if she'd never figured it out, all of my friends had. I'd been into Glow since move-in day in August.

He laughed. "Yeah, I get it. I've seen you two together a lot lately."

"I'm hoping you'll see us together more."

"If she stays..." He propped himself up more with his pillow.

"She'll stay." I wasn't going to let anything stop her.

"You sound really confident."

"I am. Very confident." I knew she could do it. She'd come so far in just a few days.

"Any particular reason?"

"I believe in her."

"Man, you've lost it." He chuckled.

"I lost it a long time ago." I put my arms behind my head.

There was a loud knock on the door. Terrance made no motion to move, so I pulled myself out of bed and walked over to it. I pulled it open, ready to react if whoever it was meant trouble.

I stepped away from the door when I saw who it was.

Mr. Wayes stepped inside the room. "I apologize for the late hour." He closed the door behind him.

Terrance shot me a confused look, but I had bigger fish to fry. "What's wrong?" My thoughts went to Glow even though I'd watched her enter the girls' hall myself.

"Nothing with Gloria," he quickly put out there. "I assure you."

"Okay, good." Relief washed over me. I wasn't surprised my thoughts had gone there first, but I was surprised with how panicked I'd become at the thought of anything happening to her.

Terrance laughed. "Not that you were worried or anything."

"Would you mind taking a walk with me, Lionel?" Mr. Wayes rested a hand on the wall as if trying to keep his balance.

"Now?" I glanced at the clock. It was close to 3 a.m.

"Yes. Does the time matter?"

I figured he would only be asking me to do this for a specific reason. Saying no wasn't really an option. "Sure. Give me a second to get dressed."

"I will meet you outside." He opened the door and walked back out, closing the door behind him.

"Okay, that was weird." Terrance looked at the closed door.

"Very, but he's got to have a reason if he's doing it." I stepped into jeans.

"And you better tell me what it is when you get back." Terrance lay back down. "But I'm not waiting up for you."

"Wouldn't expect you to." Although, I knew he'd be ready with questions. Not that I could blame him. It wasn't often that an alum showed up at your door in the middle of the night. I hurried out into the hall, through the lounge, and down the stairs. I walked into the dark night.

"Thank you for meeting me." Mr. Wayes stepped out of the shadows.

"I assume this is important." I looked out into the darkness to make sure we were really alone.

"Of course. I wouldn't have woken you up otherwise."

"You didn't wake me up."

"Thinking of Gloria, huh?" He smiled. It looked a bit eerie in the exterior lights of the dorm.

"I take it you know about us?"

"Of course." He shifted his weight from foot to foot. "And it seems like a good match."

"But that isn't why you wanted to talk to me." There was no way he'd gone through so much trouble to discuss my dating life.

"No." He shook his head. "Unfortunately not."

"Unfortunately?" My eyebrows knitted together. "Okay, that doesn't sound good."

"It's about your father."

"My father?" No. This wasn't good at all. I'd hoped he didn't even know I was related to Mathias, but that was too much to hope for.

"I don't know all the details, but I know he's been set up." Mr. Wayes rubbed the back of his neck.

"Set up?" I repeated his words. Was I missing something? "What are you talking about?"

"He's going to have to give you the full story, but there is no way he did what they said he did. He's not that reckless, and it undermines everything he's been working toward for years."

"Working toward?" Okay, maybe Mr. Wayes was crazy. "My father's been working toward something?"

"Yes. Tirelessly. I know he hasn't exactly been the best father, but he does care about our people."

"I don't think he cares about anything or anyone." It's not that I even knew him well enough to know what he cared about, but I'd never seen him do anything that wasn't selfish.

"Sometimes those closest to us are the hardest to read."

"I am not close to my father." Not by a long shot. He was more of a stranger than family.

"Maybe not now, but I do believe one day you will be. Blood runs strong."

"He abandoned my mother and me." And I would never forgive him for that. My mother deserved better.

"And he was wrong to do that." Mr. Wayes's expression was serious. "You won't hear me defending that."

"Then what are you doing?"

"Telling you that you should at least listen to him. Hear him out."

"I told him I'd see him. I'm going." Like it or not, I had no choice.

"Good." He nodded.

"Glow—Gloria is coming with me."

He rested his chin in his hand. "That may be the right decision."

"May be?" That wasn't exactly the answer I'd been hoping for.

"One never knows if a decision is right until it's played out."

"Very helpful."

"Not all true things are helpful. In fact, many of them aren't."

Did he have to talk in riddles? Why couldn't he be straight forward for a second? "So you think it's okay to bring her?" I didn't know why I was asking him, but I needed to know that I wasn't being completely irresponsible and reckless.

"Gloria can make her own decisions. If she wants to go, why not let her go?" He held out his hand palm up.

"True." It really wasn't my decision. It was hers.

"And on that note, I take your leave."

"Wait." I froze. "That's all you wanted to talk to me about? You came all the way into the dorm and got permission to get me out for that?"

"Wasn't that enough?" He wore a puzzled expression.

"All you did was tell me I should hear my father out."

"And if you heed what I say, that will be pretty significant, won't it?"

"Maybe."

"But, Lionel?"

"Yes?" I waited for what would hopefully be some useful advice.

"Be careful. Gloria's magic may be stronger than any of us know yet. She is more sensitive... well, she is more sensitive than most."

"I've sensed that too." She was special in more ways than one.

"Then I don't need to say more." He waved before disappearing back into the shadows.

I waited outside for a few more minutes before heading back up to my room. I was going to need my own morning elixir if I didn't get some sleep soon.

# GLOW

"*I* can't believe we're doing this." I looked over at Lionel from my spot in the passenger seat of his SUV.

He briefly glanced at me before returning his eyes to the road. "Neither can I. But I'm glad you're with me."

"Me too." It felt right in a way most things didn't for me. I'd spent so much of my life waiting for something to change—for me to harness my magic, for me to step up to what I was born for. It was nice for something to feel so comfortable and right so quickly, even if I didn't quite understand it.

"Yeah?" He took my hand in his. "You aren't regretting your decision yet?"

"Why would I regret it?" I pulled my leg up under me to get more comfortable.

"You did just say you can't believe you're doing this."

"Yes, but that's different from regretting it. I only meant it was hard to believe we were actually driving to one of the most notorious paranormal prisons in the U.S." I said the words in an offhanded way, but I was nervous. If I hadn't been, I'd have been worried, but I wouldn't let the nerves stop me from doing this. I was going in.

"And that's not regret?" He glanced over again.

"No. Just ruminating on it."

"Okay. I just don't want you to feel like you have to go in. You don't have to." He put his arm behind me.

I leaned into his arm. "I know. Anyway, we are supposed to be making plans." I was nervous, and when I was nervous, I needed to keep myself busy.

"I assume you mean plans for changing the rules, but I don't know if I have the mental space for that right now. I'm nervous too, but maybe for different reasons than you have."

"Your dad, huh?" I decided not to tiptoe around things. Sometimes being forward was the best way. "When is the last time you saw him?"

"It's been years." Lionel ran his hand down my back.

"And now you're going to see him like this... I'm sorry." What an awful way to have a reunion.

"Don't be sorry. You're keeping me company, which helps. I just hope this doesn't blow up in my face."

"You said Mr. Wayes told you to listen to your dad." He'd only mentioned their conversation, and we'd been so preoccupied with my magic that I hadn't asked many questions. A realization hit me. I'd been acting super self-absorbed. "What do you think that was about?" I'd originally kept my questions to a minimum, but if it helped Lionel to talk about it, there was no reason not to get my questions answered. And we needed to keep the conversation on him. I was done monopolizing.

"I have no clue. He was all mysterious about it, but he did say it was some sort of set up, and that my father revealing himself in the way he allegedly did would have undermined what he had worked for. As far as I knew, my dad didn't work for much of anything other than a paycheck he didn't share with us."

I reached for his hand and took it in mine. "I'm sure that must have been hard. Growing up with a dad like that, I mean."

"My mom was amazing. She worked like crazy, yet was always there for me. She pretty much gave up her whole life to raise me, and I'll never be able to repay her."

"I think living your life to the fullest is the best thing you can do. I'm not a mom, but I'd think that's what she'd want the most."

"What are your parents like?" He stroked my hand with his thumb.

"My parents?" I thought about his question. "Hmm. They are pretty normal, I guess. Well, normal for two wolf-warlock hybrids."

"So you have two hybrids as parents?" His thumb pushed down harder. It felt so good.

"Uh-huh. So, I shouldn't be struggling so much with the magic. Most of the time, it's only an issue when you are one and one."

"Well, fitting the norm is overrated." He moved our entwined hands to his lap.

I laughed. "What about you? I know your dad is a hybrid from watching the news, but your mom?"

"Wolf. She was in Wolf Born."

"Oh. Wow. How does she feel about you being in bound?" Both my parents were bound, so it wasn't something I'd ever really thought about. Was it strange when your child was in a different house?

"She's just glad she could afford to get me here. Even with the scholarships..."

"Sorry. I mean I'm on a scholarship too. Well, and my grandmother is helping a bit." She was helping more than a bit. She'd also been bound, and I was her only grandchild. Keeping the family tradition alive was a pretty big deal to her.

"That's cool. Are you close to your grandmother?"

"I was." As a little girl I'd spent every spare moment at her house. "But you know, it's harder now with being so far away."

"Where are you from again? Up north, right?"

"Pennsylvania. A small town about forty-five minutes outside of Philadelphia." No one knew the name of my town, so there was no reason to explain it that way.

"I've never been to Philadelphia. Worth taking a trip sometime?"

"Yeah. Absolutely. Lots of history and good food. Plus, you can tie it into doing New York at the same time. Lots to do."

"All right. Is that going to be our next road trip?" He released my hand and settled his hand on my leg. Even through my jeans, I felt the warmth of his touch.

"That would be a long road trip." Not that it was impossible, but it wasn't a short little trip.

"How do you get home, then? Do you fly?" He cared. He actually cared what I did. At least that was how he came across.

"I flew home for winter break. I stayed here for Thanksgiving to save money."

"Wait. What?" He slowed the car. "How didn't I know that? I would have invited you to join me and my mom. I grew up only an hour from campus."

"I didn't tell anyone for that reason. I got permission to stay in the dorm."

"You should have told me." There was a twinge of something sour in his voice. Hurt. Regret. I wasn't sure what.

"We barely knew each other."

"Well, we would have gotten to know each other over turkey and dressing."

"Dressing? You mean, stuffing right?"

He groaned. "Please tell me you don't call Coke pop."

"No, it's soda." I grinned.

"And what do you call the shoes you wear to play sports?"

"Sneakers." I laughed. "I call them sneakers."

"They are called tennis shoes just for future reference."

"Why? I'm not using them for tennis," I teased. It hadn't taken me long at Lunar Academy to get used to the southern terms for things.

"Okay, here we go. One more test."

"I'm ready." I twisted more in my seat so I could look at him.

"What's it called when you make hot dogs and hamburgers on the grill?"

I knew what answer he was looking for, but I also knew it would be really fun to walk into it. "A barbecue."

"Oh, no. You didn't."

I laughed. "Come on. I had to go there."

"You're lucky you are so damn cute." He squeezed my leg.

"Otherwise what?"

"I don't know. Just you're lucky."

I mussed up his hair. "You're funny."

"Not funny looking, I hope."

"Nope. Not funny looking." I ran my hand down his cheek. "You don't know how handsome you are, do you?"

"Handsome?" He leaned into my hand. "I'm not handsome."

"See. I was right. You don't know."

"I'm not saying I'm bad looking, but handsome is something different."

"I don't know what your definition of handsome is, but my definition for sure covers you no matter what you think." He was classically handsome with a touch of rustic to make him seem completely unreal. Like he belonged on a box advertising some outdoor product rather than sitting behind the wheel of the car I was currently a passenger in.

"Well, you're beautiful." He put his hand on my cheek. "And damn, you have the softest skin ever."

"Thank you." I closed my eyes and enjoyed the sensation of his hand. "See, that's how you take a compliment."

"Because you know you're beautiful. You can't act like it's the same thing."

"And you know you're handsome." I refused to believe he didn't realize he was good-looking. That was one of those things you just figured out.

"And you're rich with magic. Once you get the hang of it, you'll be better than anyone."

"Nope." I wasn't going to take a false compliment. I was so behind on getting my powers that it wasn't even funny.

"And I thought you could take a compliment."

"I can." When they were real. It was not like I thought I was the most beautiful girl or anything. I wasn't. I was quite plain in a lot of ways, but I could at least believe he thought I was beautiful. That was the difference. There was a true possibility he believed it, and that was really what a compliment was. Someone expressing what they believed about you.

"Then why aren't you saying thanks?"

"This is entirely different. It's not true." I didn't want to have to break down my philosophy on this.

He laughed dryly. "I see how it is. You are confident in your looks, but not in your magical ability?"

"Oh my gosh, you are making me sound so conceited." Maybe I would have to explain it.

"Well, clearly you know you're hot."

I swatted at his arm. "No, I do not."

"I called you beautiful, and you said thank you. I tell you that you are powerful, and you say no."

"Because I wish I were powerful. That's more important to me than beauty." And power wasn't in the eye of the beholder. Power either was or was not there.

"You are both. Completely both." His eyes locked on mine for a moment, maybe a moment too long given he was driving, before he returned his gaze to the road.

"So are you."

"I'm beautiful?" His lips twisted into a lopsided grin.

"Yeah, in a guy way."

"Beautiful in a guy way and handsome. Next thing you're going to do is call me sexy."

I laughed. "Well, you are that too." Might as well keep going with the truth.

"Thank you. That's what you want from me, right? For me to learn to accept a compliment."

"Pretty much. Yeah." And to understand how unbelievably attracted I was to him. Even though it went well beyond looks. I wasn't sure I was ready to admit that part yet.

"Your turn." He settled his hand back on my leg.

"Okay."

"You are beautiful and powerful."

I was ready to give my answer this time. "Thank you."

"Thank you." He patted my leg.

"Why are you saying thank you now?" Was I missing something?

"Because I know that was hard for you."

"It may get easier when I can actually use magic." I was getting close, but I wasn't there yet. If I ever got there.

"Which you can. You found that book."

"That wasn't using magic. That was locating something."

"And how did you locate it?" He tapped his fingers on my leg.

"Wait." A sickening feeling built in my stomach. "But if that's using magic, then why is you being able to sense me through magic breaking the rules?"

"Because they can't punish me for doing something I can't help. Right? I mean obviously they can, but it's not something I can turn off. You'll realize that soon enough."

"So you think I'll be able to start sensing other magic stuff?"

"Absolutely. Mr. Wayes was actually a little bit nervous about you coming with me because of that. I mean to the prison."

"What do you mean?" Now this was news to me. And information that might have been helpful before we were hours into our drive.

"He thinks you may be really sensitive, and well, there's a lot of stuff in there."

"But he still thought I should come?" I tried not to be worried. I mean, if I did sense things, that would be a good thing.

"He said the decision was yours, and if you want to stay in the car, you definitely can still do that, you know?"

"I'm going inside. We've already discussed that."

"I know. I'm just making sure you know it."

But maybe he wasn't asking for me. "You want me to, right?"

"I do." He took my hand. "And maybe that's weird, but I'm getting really used to having you around with me."

I was getting used to it too. "Do you want me to drive some? I don't mind."

"Nah. I mean I appreciate you offering, but four hours isn't a long drive for me."

"I know. But this is a stressful drive... not the road." It was really just open interstate mostly at seventy miles per hour. There was almost no traffic, so we couldn't complain about that. "But where we're going."

"Thankfully, I have the best company." He covered my hand with his.

"The best?" I kissed his cheek. "You may be pushing your luck there."

"You are. If nothing else, you've done a fantastic job distracting me."

"Have I? Because that's what I was fixin' to do."

He cracked up. "Okay. That was well played."

"Ready to admit not all Northerners are bad?"

"I never said they were bad. I merely suggested our vernacular was preferable."

"Bless your heart."

He busted out laughing. "Dear lord, babe. That was too perfect. See? This is what I mean. You're the best kind of company."

Babe? He hadn't called me that before. I kind of liked it. I more than kind of liked it. I smiled. Very happy with myself. "No one can accuse me of lacking a sense of humor."

"Hot, smart, powerful, and funny. Could I possibly do better?"

"Probably. But let's not worry about that now."

"Can I ask you something, Glow?" He made small circles on my hand with his thumb.

"Of course you can ask. That doesn't mean I'll answer." One had to be careful before agreeing to something like that.

"Aren't you a spitfire today?"

"Is that your question?" I knew it wasn't, but sometimes it was impossible not to tease. It came so naturally with him.

"No, it's not. My question is whether you were into me before a few days ago."

"Oh, wow." I hadn't been expecting that one.

He laughed. "Is that a hard question to answer or something?"

"Actually, yes. It's a really hard question to answer." And not one I wanted to. I wasn't sure what I could tell him that would be the truth, yet wouldn't ruin everything.

"Okay. Why?"

"Because it's not so clear cut."

"Meaning what?" He was looking straight ahead.

"Meaning I always thought you were cute."

"Just cute?"

"Hot." Sexy as hell really, but there was no reason to go overboard.

"But nothing about my sparkling personality?"

"I didn't really know your sparkling personality." I had been focused on my lack of magic. I got to know Penny, but that was because she pushed so hard for me to let her in. I definitely wouldn't have gone out of my way to bond with him if I'd been left to my own devices.

"And you didn't want to know me?"

"I was focused on other things."

"And you had other things to focus on. I'll give you that." He took his hand away and put it on the wheel. I missed the touch immediately and tried not to read into it. Maybe he just preferred to drive that way,

"What about you?" I pushed away my worries. I couldn't make a huge deal about it, considering what we were getting ready to walk into.

"What about me?"

"Come on. You know what I mean. Did you like me?"

"Of course. Why else did I show up at Convenience? I already told you I was intimidated, yet looking for an opening."

"Yeah. But why did you like me?" I'd had a few boyfriends over the years, but not many.

"You mean aside from physical attraction?"

"Yeah." Although, it was nice to know he'd been attracted to me before.

"You just always seemed cool. Special."

"Well, I'm definitely special." I forced a laugh.

He laughed in a more natural way. "Ah, yes, you are. In more ways than one." His expression turned serious. "But really, I appreciate you coming with me. I can't really believe it, to be honest."

"Hopefully, I don't get in the way."

"Why would you be in the way?"

"You know. What if Mr. Wayes is right? And I'm super sensitive? What if I freak out or get weird or something?"

"You won't."

"How do you know that?"

"Because I do. You will stay in control. You can do anything." His confidence in me was great and all, but I didn't really understand it.

"And you would make a great motivational speaker."

He laughed.

"I'm serious. I literally heard your voice in my head the other day, telling me to find a better spot. And you heard me in class. I'm even quoting you now."

"If I can't practice magic, I might as well help you do it. Right?"

"That's totally not the same thing." And I felt awful. What the academy was doing to him was unfair.

"Not the same thing, but close enough." He returned his hand to my leg, pushing away my worries.

*A*lmandy Shifter Prison looked just as foreboding as I'd expected. It wasn't just the barbed wire on the fence—that was more for show than anything- it was also the magic I could feel even from my seat in my car, and the half-vamps standing watch at evenly spaced intervals around the perimeter.

I pulled up to the gate.

"State your business," a guard, dressed in an army fatigue uniform, barked from his place in the guard house.

"We are here to visit Mathias Pillar. We prearranged this appointment." I tried to stay calm. It wouldn't help anything if I came across as nervous, even though I sure as hell was.

"Name?" The guard's expression never changed.

"Lionel Daniels."

"And her?" He pointed a finger at Glow.

"Gloria Mayer," she answered before I could.

"IDs." There was no please. No formalities. Nothing. He was all seriousness.

Glow pulled her license out of her wallet and handed it to me. I put it with mine and handed them over.

The guard scanned them with something before handing them back. "Visiting time is only until four o'clock."

I glanced at my watch. It wasn't even eleven. "We'll be out of here way before that." I planned to keep this meeting very, very short.

"I repeat. Visiting time is only until four o'clock." The guard's expression never wavered.

"Got it." I handed Glow her license. "Are we clear to drive in?"

"Yes. But you will have to go through multiple levels of security. The magic is strong on the both of you."

I glanced at Glow to make sure she'd heard him.

"We understand." I made eye contact with the guard.

He nodded and opened the gate.

I slowly drove through.

Glow grabbed my hand. I wasn't sure if she was taking it for me or for her, but either way, I enjoyed the feel of her hand in mine.

The drive leading to the parking lot was lined with barbed wire as well; the fences went so high it was almost dizzying to look on either side of the narrow road.

"So, they are really up on security here." Glow looked out her window. "It's pretty crazy."

"Which is probably a good thing. You know, considering who's in here." It wasn't publicly reported who was held inside the walls of this prison, but that didn't mean people didn't know.

"Yeah." Glow visibly shook. "You're right."

"You really don't have to do this. There's still time for you to change your mind." Even as I said it, I knew she had to go in with me. I'd be worried sick about her if I left her in the car.

"Yes, I do."

I pulled into a parking spot. "Fine, but we stay together the whole time."

"Yes. I just really hope I don't have to go to the bathroom while we're in there." She didn't crack a smile, so I assumed she was really worried about it.

"If you do, I'll wait right outside." I didn't want to come across as totally overprotective, but we were going into a maximum security paranormal prison. This place was no joke.

"Thanks. And I'm here for you too." She kissed my cheek.

I needed more than that kind of kiss. My lips found hers, and I let all of my worries disappear as I focused on her mouth. And then her neck. She moaned as my lips moved down her neck. She arched into me, and I took that as an invitation to continue my lips' trail downward.

Then, she abruptly pushed me away. "That feels amazing and all, but we need to get this over with. Plus, how long is it going to be before someone comes over to see why we're still sitting in the car?"

"You're right." I reluctantly pulled away. "But we can pick up where we left off tonight."

"Sounds perfect." She brushed her lips against mine before pulling away before I could start things up again.

I got out of the car and met her around her side. I slipped my hand around hers before we walked toward the entrance to the dark stone building.

Neither of us said a word as we neared the entrance. Any excitement from the road trip part of the day had disappeared

"Bag." Another guard dressed in the same fatigues as the guy in the gate house pointed to Glow's small backpack.

She held it out. "Here."

The guard looked inside and then spilled the contents on a table.

I tried not to watch as he went through the papers and other odds and ends he found. It felt like an invasion of privacy even if a stranger was now sorting through it.

"Why are you researching late-blooming magic?" The guard held up a pile of papers. I couldn't really believe she had articles printed out, but it did fit in with her old school way of taking notes by hand.

"Because I'm a late bloomer of magic." Glow held out her hand. "I can take all that back now."

The guard studied her. "You have plenty of magic."

"Whatever." She looked away. "Could I please have my bag back?"

The guard rifled through more papers and even opened the cap of a pen.

"Does it matter what she's researching?" I didn't see how any of this affected whether we could go inside.

He lowered the papers and looked at me. "We need to make sure she isn't here to cause a riot."

"Because late-blooming magic could cause a riot?" Glow frowned. "You've got to be kidding me."

He didn't laugh. "You never know what's going to cause a riot."

Glow sighed. "I'm not here to start a riot."

"Then why are you here?" He started to put her stuff back in her bag.

"She's here to visit my father with me," I quickly explained.

"Why?" The guard paused with a packet of tissues in his hand.

"Because that's a normal thing for a girlfriend to do with her boyfriend." Gloria winced as the guard dropped a lipstick on the concrete floor. "Isn't it?"

Girlfriend? Boyfriend? I liked the sound of that. I realized she was saying it to help our situation, but that didn't mean I couldn't enjoy the way it made me feel.

The guard picked up the lipstick. "If you're lying, there will be severe consequences."

"You mean beyond being in the middle of prison riot?" She shook her head. "If I'm lying, I'll have big problems. I get it. I assure you I have enough problems already. We're going to see his father. That's it. Now, if you could get the rest of the check over with, preferably without dropping more of my stuff, so we could get on with our visit, that would be great."

The guard wrinkled the paper as he pushed them

back into her bag. "I'm the one setting the pace here. Not you. You don't get to tell me what to do."

"Fine. Then tell us what to do. But we really want to get in so we can get out."

"Is she always this pushy?" The guard looked to me.

I shrugged. "Isn't it wonderful?"

"Wonderful?" He coughed. "You couldn't pay me enough to put up with that kind of lip even if she is easy on the eyes."

"Easy on the eyes?" Glow's face turned red. "Because that's professional."

The guard scowled. "I'd get your girlfriend to calm down if you ever want to get in to see your father."

"Listen. I'm sorry." Glow let out a slow breath. "I just don't like being belittled. You'll get to stop listening to me though, if you let us through."

"True." He pulled out two metal wands that looked an awful lot like what they use at an airport and wove them over her. It beeped like crazy. "A lot of magic in you. You better not cause trouble."

"I won't." She stepped away.

He used the wands on me next. They beeped again. "Two of you with all that magic. I can't imagine what kind of offspring you'd have together."

"Well, that's a long way off," Gloria quickly replied.

I noticed she didn't say never. Once again, I knew it was likely just to help our case, but it was still interesting to hear. Not that I was thinking about having kids with her yet either. Or I hadn't been until he mentioned it.

The guard held onto her backpack. "I expect the two

of you will stay out of trouble while you are inside. I also need your phone." He looked at me.

"That's the plan," I answered before Glow could say anything. I found her responses to the guy humorous, but I didn't want anything else to slow us down. The sooner we got inside and to my dad, the sooner we could get out. I handed over my phone even though going in without a way to contact the outside world made me nervous.

Glow stayed glued to my side as we made our way through the winding corridors of the prison. The walk was mostly quiet until we reached a hall full of prison cells. The bars rattled as we walked past, and both men and women yelled taunts at us. There were also plenty of catcalls that were mostly for Glow, but a few seemed like they were for me. I put my arm around her. I hoped she knew I'd protect her—no matter what the cost. Not that she couldn't protect herself. Her magic may have come in late, but she was a wolf. She had plenty of strength in that form. But most of these prisoners were powerful too. Many more powerful than us.

"Come a little closer, little lady," someone called from a cell. "Let me see that pretty face."

My wolf growled, but I tried to keep him in control. Nothing good was going to come out of me attacking someone. My no-magic ban at school would be the least of my problems.

"Do you feel that?" Glow whispered.

"What exactly? I feel all sorts of things." None of them good. Discomfort and unease were the two best descriptors that came to mind.

"That magic. It feels awful." She walked faster.

"I feel some sort of magic, but what are you feeling?" Her voice was strained, and that had me really worried. "Can you describe it?"

"It just tastes dark."

"Tastes?" Mr. Wayes's warning came back to me. He'd predicted she'd be particularly sensitive, and now it appeared he was absolutely right. "What do you mean by tastes?" I couldn't jump to conclusions.

"You can't taste it? That awful metallic tinge in your mouth?" She made a disgusted motion with her mouth.

Wow. I'd heard of those who could taste magic, but I'd never met one. Mr. Wayes was right about Glow's magic being off the charts. "I can't taste it, but I am sure you can. When did it start?"

"When we turned down this hall." She stuck out her tongue.

"Okay. I'd say we should turn around and go, but at this point, I don't know how to do that." I glanced over my shoulder to see we were still being followed by two guards. We were trailing a third.

"We have to see your father anyway. Otherwise, we're going to have to come back." She shivered.

"You're right." We continued walking, and Glow shook again at my side. I looked at her pained face. I wasn't sure how much of it was fear and how much of it was the taste. "You okay, babe?"

"I'm fine." She leaned into my side. "But the taste is still there." She spoke in barely a whisper, but I knew if anyone wanted to, they could hear her. Shifters had superior hearing.

"Let's try to keep that between us." Hopefully, she understood the warning in my words. I wanted her to be open with me, but I also didn't want her attracting any more attention than she already was. Mr. Wayes had been wrong. I never should have brought her here, even if it's what she wanted. I should have done a better job protecting her by keeping her away. Hopefully, whatever the bad magic was, it wouldn't be directed at us. We'd wronged nobody, but generally speaking, that didn't mean anything.

We turned down a dark hall. The lights were so dim even my night vision did little to help.

It was also silent aside from an occasional scream.

Glow grabbed onto my arm. "This is horrible. Absolutely horrible."

"I know. I am so sorry you are dealing with this. I hope you eventually forgive me." I looked up at a light that was blinking every few seconds, creating a strobe effect. We needed to get out of that hallway and fast.

"I'm the one who volunteered to come. None of this is your fault."

No matter what she said I felt guilty, but that guilt wasn't going to help me now. The best thing I could do was focus on keeping my guard up so there were no surprises. I knew that would be easier said than done.

We made it down the rest of the corridor and turned again. I'd tried to keep track of all of the turns, but we'd made so many and it was so dark, it was getting harder.

"Right through here." A guard inserted a key into a set of steel bar-covered metal doors, and he pulled the double set open. He gestured for us to step through.

Glow and I exchanged looks. Neither of us wanted to take a single step through there.

## GLOW

The taste of metal was growing worse by the minute. All I wanted to do was turn around and run, but I knew that wasn't an option. Besides, turning back would still mean going back through those horrible halls again.

I caught Lionel's eyes as the two iron doors opened for us. The taste was so bad, I wanted to vomit, but what choice did we have? We had to walk through. Still, I clutched Lionel's hand like it was a lifeline.

We stepped through the door, and I was immediately hit with relief. The taste disappeared, and I let out a huge sigh. "Thank you."

"You seem better," Lionel whispered.

"I am. It's gone."

"Okay. Good." He rubbed my back. "We'll just have to be careful on our way out."

"I thought it was going to be worse."

"So did I. But let's stay alert." Lionel glanced over his

shoulder, presumably at the two guards following us. I knew I was getting weirded out by being followed.

"Absolutely." He was right. Staying alert was important. What if I was being lulled into a sense of security? A false sense of security. This whole thing was crazy. How could I actually taste magic? That doesn't make sense for someone like me who couldn't even wield magic.

We made our way down the much brighter corridor. This area of the prison was newer, or it at least appeared to be. The floors were clean, the walls bright white. There were rooms with doors rather than cells, and I assumed these were offices and things. The lighting was bright and welcoming. If this was the visitor area, couldn't they have had a door that let us straight in here? Why make visitors go through all that hell just to get there?

The front guard stopped short when we reached another set of double doors that were also covered in steel bars. "Beyond this point, you will be on your own."

"Uh, why?" We'd been accompanied by three guards this far. I understood if they couldn't all stay with us, but why drop us down to none?

"Because of policy." He shifted his weight from foot to foot. What was with these guards and their attitude? Their emotionless voices? It was beginning to feel it was part of the requirement to have their position or something.

"Is my father through there?" Lionel pointed to the door.

The guard nodded. "You'll find him."

"What the hell is that supposed to mean?" Lionel snapped. He'd been so calm up to this point that the switch was palpable.

"It means you'll find him." The guard frowned. "It shouldn't be too hard for you magic sorts."

"Is that why you can't go through? Part of some spell set up or something?" Lionel asked.

"We are pure wolf. We don't go in there." One of the other guards had backed up a ways down the hall, back toward the way we'd come.

"Then why not send us with a hybrid guard? Like the one up front?" It seemed unwise to send visitors into part of the prison by themselves. Hadn't that front guard been concerned about a riot?

"You act like we have lots of extra magic hybrids sitting around. Most of your sort don't choose the prison jobs. Too uncomfortable. Why do you think Gary chooses to work the front? It keeps him from the crazies." The guard wrinkled his nose. I assumed Gary was the jerk up front who threw around my stuff.

"The crazies?" I wasn't going to let another guard disrespect me, even if it wasn't about me specifically, but my kind. "Watch it."

"You haven't met these wolves."

"Is my father the only one in there?" Lionel eyed the door again.

The guard laughed. "Are you serious? You think he has a whole wing to himself?"

"A whole wing?" They were making us enter a whole

wing of the prison alone?

"Yes." The third guard nodded. "We've been bringing in more and more hybrids lately. It's almost like an epidemic."

Lionel and I once again exchanged looks. An epidemic of crime-committing hybrids? Usually, the magic sort could protect themselves from trouble. Why were they allowing themselves to fall into custody so easily? It didn't make sense, but it couldn't be a good thing.

"Will we be safe in there?' Lionel looked between the three guards.

"I can't make any promises. I guess it depends how strong your magic is." The first guard stepped around us and joined the other guards.

"That's not good enough." Lionel clenched his jaw.

"They wouldn't be sending a couple of kids in if they didn't think you'd come out alive." The third guard checked his watch.

Alive? What about barely alive? That didn't sound good either. "Fine. We've come this far." I knew Lionel was right about letting our guard down, but the fact that I couldn't taste the dark magic anymore had to mean something. At least I hoped it did.

"Here is the key." The first guard held out a small metal key.

I let Lionel take it. After all, we were there to see his father.

"Give us a two-minute head start." The second guard started down the hall, and the other two followed.

"Are they really this scared?" I asked. "It's crazy."

"Non-magics get freaked out by magic." Lionel turned the key in his hand. "But are you okay? You want to do this?"

"Of course. What do you want me to do instead? Turn around and go back through that hell hall by myself?" I shivered.

"No, I don't." He sighed. "I really am sorry I dragged you into this."

I took his free hand. "Stop. You didn't drag me. Okay? I volunteered for this. I'm here of my own free will. Stop with the guilt."

"Okay. I'll try." He opened his palm, revealing the key. "I'm going to open this door. If things get weird, we turn around. Okay?"

I nodded, even though turning around was the last thing on my mind. I needed time before I faced that awful hallway again. I tried to forget about the screams and the taste as Lionel inserted the key and the lock fell away.

"All right, last chance to change your mind."

"Stop." I frowned.

"Okay. But we have no clue what we are going to find on the other side of the doors."

"No. But that's life. You never know what's coming." I'd learned that truth a long time ago.

"This is a little bit crazier than normal life."

"True. But it doesn't mean we can turn around."

"Okay. Let's get this over with." He looked at me, and I nodded again before he pushed the doors open.

We stepped through the doorway, and the metallic taste was back with a vengeance. I doubled over as the doors slammed closed.

"Glow, you okay?" Lionel helped me stand up.

"We have to get out of here." I barely got the words out. The taste was overwhelming, and it was no longer just in my mouth. It was seeping down my throat.

There were no handles on the doors. They were merely metal panels. Lionel tried to pry them open with his hands, but nothing happened.

"Shit." I let the curse slip out. "What do we do?"

"We can use magic." Lionel put his arms around me from behind to help me stand.

"No! You'll get in trouble." I knew we were in a really bad situation, but I couldn't let him get kicked out of the Lunar Academy.

"Who the hell cares if I get in trouble at the academy? I feel it now. This is bad." He let out an audible breath. "Let me come up with something."

"I wish I could use my magic." I coughed. The taste seeped deeper inside me. I was going to choke.

"Maybe you can. But we can't wait."

"Son?"

Lionel turned around, which meant I turned with him. We came face-to-face with a man with long brown hair and a red bushy beard that went halfway to his chest. He was wearing a white jumpsuit.

"Mathias." Lionel's voice was cold.

"I told you to call me father. Or dad. Or anything but that." Mathias took a step closer to us.

"And I'm not listening to you. I am here. What do you want?" Lionel tensed.

"Let's find a place to sit down." Mathias gestured for us to move farther into the hallway. The choking sensation had lessened, and I finally looked around. The floors and walls of this part of the prison were a deep brown, and the lighting wasn't bright, but it was nothing like the hell hall. But why had the taste gone away so suddenly? Did it have to do with Mathias? It sure had timed up with his arrival.

Mathias's lips twisted into a smile as his eyes settled on my face. "And who is this?"

"No one you need to concern yourself with." Lionel's arms tightened around me. "I'm here to talk to you. It's me you requested. She's going to join us, but leave her alone."

"Oh, come now. You brought her with you. Surely you wanted me to meet her." Mathias smiled at me, and I knew somehow he was the reason the taste had disappeared. He was helping somehow.

"My name is Gloria, sir." The man had helped me. The least I could do was introduce myself.

"Pleasure to meet you, Gloria." Mathias held out a hand toward me.

I accepted the handshake. His hand was cold and clammy, but I hoped I managed to hide my reaction. "Nice to meet you, Mr. Pillar."

Lionel's hands released my waist, and I stepped to the side.

Mathias turned his attention to Lionel. "You have

good taste in women, son."

"That isn't what you wanted to talk about."

"No, it wasn't." Mathias nodded. "But there is no reason a man can't talk to his son about his girlfriend."

Lionel put his arm around me. "I'm only your son when it's convenient for you."

"I admit I wasn't there for you, but I did it for your own good. For your mother's good. I wasn't meant to be a father."

"Then why did you become one?" Lionel snapped.

"I have to assume you already know how babies are made, son." Mathias's eyes danced with amusement.

"Stop calling me son." A vein in Lionel's neck popped up. He was growing angry. If he wasn't careful, his wolf might come out.

"Why? Why does that bother you so much?" Mathias seemed to be searching his son's face for answers.

Lionel's hands balled into fists at his side. "Because it does. And what you are saying is you knocked mom up and then didn't want me. Great. Well, you want me now. Might as well tell me why."

"Let's sit. Like civilized people."

"We aren't civilized people, though." Lionel ran his hand up and down my back in an absentminded way.

He was angry. I understood why, but it was still so hard to witness. I wanted to help him, but I didn't know how. But no matter how mad Lionel was, we'd come here for a reason. Even Mr. Wayes said Lionel had to listen to his father. "Maybe we should sit down. We're here, so we might as well have the conversation we came for." I

115

hoped Lionel didn't get mad at me for siding with his dad. I was doing what I knew I had to.

"I knew I liked this one." Mathias smiled at me. "Very well said."

"Fine. We can sit." Lionel rubbed the back of his neck.

I grabbed Lionel's hand. This whole experience had been crazy, but we could get through this part too. I was still so grateful the horrible taste had subsided.

"Right this way." Mathias waved us on with both his hands.

"We might as well hear him out," I whispered to Lionel. I knew Mathias probably heard me, but I had to get Lionel to cool down enough to listen if we were ever getting out of there.

Mathias led us farther down the brown-walled hall. There was nothing there until we turned a corner, and then there was a row of cells. I peeked inside one and saw someone sleeping in a bed. In the next cell a woman stared at the wall. Her eyes were wide open, but it looked like she was in a trance.

Mathias walked to the end, and stopped in front of the last cell. "Come on in. Check out my place."

"You expect us to sit with you in your jail cell?" Lionel shook his head. "You are even crazier than I thought."

"Is there somewhere else you'd rather talk?" Mathias slipped through the narrow opening between the end of the bars and the wall. "I have a perfectly good table in here. I even brewed some tea."

I stepped closer to the bars and looked into the cell. Well, it was a cell because there were bars outside of it, but really it looked more like a studio apartment with a kitchenette and everything. The only other thing that screamed prison was that there was a toilet out in the open. This wasn't what I expected from a cell in a maximum security prison, but it was not like I'd ever even been inside a paranormal prison before and they weren't depicted on TV or anything.

"Tea?" Lionel hung back behind me. "You made tea?"

"Yes. I've stopped drinking coffee. I think tea is the healthier option." Mathias pulled out a chair. "Here. Gloria, take a seat. I'll find us some biscuits."

I looked back at Lionel and then at the cell. We weren't going to get anywhere if we stood outside the cell and stared. I walked in.

Lionel grabbed my hand to stop me. "Biscuits? Last time I checked, you weren't British."

"I thought you didn't know me at all." Mathias wore an amused smile.

"I don't. But I know you were born in Mississippi, not London."

"You remember where I was born?"

I used this calm in their conversation to walk into the cell while still holding Lionel's hand so he followed in with me. At least we were getting somewhere.

"Yes. Why does that matter?" Lionel looked around, as if surprised he'd blindly followed me in.

"Because it means you care." Mathias's voice got low.

Not like a whisper, but like with an understated emphasis.

Lionel groaned. "Come on, Mathias. Get to the point."

"I will once you both sit down and I get everyone set with tea and biscuits." He pulled out a tin from a cabinet.

I took a seat and patted the chair next to me. Lionel sat down and made the universal sign for crazy. I shrugged. Who defined crazy anyway? I was giving Mathias a lot of credit, but I was still convinced he was the one who saved me from the metallic magic taste, so he was definitely in my good graces.

"Chocolate biscuits?" Mathias placed the tin in front of me.

"Oh, sure." I wasn't hungry at all, but I wasn't going to be rude. I would at least take one, whether I ate it or not.

Mathias sat down across from us and poured three cups of tea. He passed them out.

I made no move to touch the tea. I knew it would go straight through me and I'd have to use the bathroom, and I certainly wasn't using the open one in his cell.

Mathias wrapped his hands around his mug. "I should have said this earlier, but thank you for coming, Lionel. And thank you for coming as well, Gloria. It's a pleasure to meet someone who clearly cares deeply about my son."

I did care about him, even if I still barely knew him. It definitely didn't feel that way anymore.

"What do you want to talk about?" Lionel crossed his

arms.

"Aren't you going to drink your tea?" Mathias brought his mug to his lips.

"Maybe later." Lionel made no move to touch his mug.

"You need to drink your tea." Mathias lowered his voice to a whisper. "Please." His eyes were wide, and there was something akin to panic in them.

"Why? What did you do to the tea?" Lionel straightened in his seat. "Tell me now."

"The tea is safe. I promise. Gloria, please. Believe me. You need to drink the tea, and you need to drink it fast. Even just a few sips." Mathias put his hands together as if pleading.

"No fucking way." Lionel slammed his fist on the table.

"Remember what Mr. Wayes said..." I tried to gently remind Lionel. I didn't want to get into the middle of anything, but I felt like I had to say something.

"Mr. Wayes? You two have been talking to Adam?" Mathias looked between us.

"I work for him." I left it at that. I wasn't going to give more details than what he asked for.

"He told you then? Told you what happened to me?" Mathias ran a hand through his long hair.

"He told me it wasn't true. What they accused you of." Lionel rested his elbows in front of him. "But that you would tell me the details."

"And I will. After you drink the tea. But you need to drink it. I swear it's for your own good."

"Why?" I asked. "If you told us why, we'd drink it."

"I can't tell you why. I shouldn't even be telling you to drink it." He stood and walked over to the entrance to his cell. He slid the bars closed the whole way.

"Hey, hey. What are you doing?" Lionel shot out of his chair. "You had better not be locking us in here."

"Of course not." Mathias stood in front of the bars, blocking Lionel. "I'm trying to protect you."

"Protect us from what?" Lionel huffed.

"What's out there." Mathias put his hands on the bars and looked out.

"What are you talking about?" Lionel shook his head. "And if it's so dangerous here, why did you insist I come? None of this makes sense."

"Because you are the only one I can trust. They are trying to drive me insane." He released the bars and turned back around.

Lionel's expression softened a little. "No offense, Mathias, but you seem insane already."

"If I don't get out of here soon, I will be."

"Please, try to explain." I was starting to get increasingly freaked out. I stayed seated even though the other two were now standing. I figured maybe if I kept calm it would rub off on them.

"This is all a set up." Mathias resumed his seat at the table. "All of this."

"All of what?" I leaned forward on one elbow.

"This whole thing." Mathias spread his arms out wide. "This wing for hybrids."

"A setup for whom? By whom?" Lionel took his seat

beside me. At least that plan had worked. I had them both at the table again. Figuratively and literally, that seemed increasingly important.

"Drink the tea and I'll tell you anything." Mathias pushed our mugs closer to us.

"We are not drinking the damn tea." Lionel pushed his back to where it was.

"Why not?" Mathias frowned. "Gloria, please. I worry about you. You need to drink it."

"How do we know it's safe?" I didn't want to anger the guy, but it was also a completely fair question.

"How are you feeling right now, Gloria?" Mathias looked into my eyes. "Tell me. Be honest."

"Better. Much better."

"And why do you think you're feeling better?"

"It's something you did." It had to be. "Right?"

"Yes." He nodded. "See."

Lionel groaned again. "Bullshit."

"It's not." Once again, I wished I didn't have to get in the middle of this father-son dispute, but I had to be honest. "It got better when he showed up."

"Which means he may have created the problem to begin with."

"But I had the issue before we entered this wing." It had been awful in the hell hall, and that was so far away from Mathias, there was no way it was him.

"But not as bad," Lionel pointed out.

"Still. I believe him." I did.

"I am putting up a wall for you. It can't hold forever, and it's all going to hit you again."

"Can the tea protect me from that?" I'd guzzle the whole pot if that was the case. I never wanted to experience that awful taste again.

"Not the way you want it to, but what's coming will be worse. Drink the tea so we can talk, and I can help you both escape before it's too late."

Something about his words rang true, and I decided to take a risk. A big risk I knew I might regret for the rest of my life. But I went with it anyway. I picked up the mug.

"Glow, don't." Lionel reached for mug. "You can't drink that."

"We have to trust him." I held the mug away from him. "You know it." I sipped the tea. And it tasted like tea. Like Chamomile tea—but not the usual kind. The kind of tea my grandmother always made for me." And it hit me. I understood. "I know what this is."

"Do you?" There was excitement in Mathias's voice.

"This is truth-seer tea." There was no question. I'd have known that taste anywhere.

"It is." Mathias smiled. "You figured it out."

I took another sip. "Lionel, it's safe. My grandmother used to make this for me when I was little. She said it was good to get used to seeing the truth in anything."

"It is. The truth can be frightening, but that doesn't make it less important." Mathias was starting to sound an awful lot like my grandmother.

Lionel picked up his mug. "You sure about this, Glow?"

"Yes. I'd know this taste anywhere."

Lionel took a sip of his tea. "Okay. We are drinking our tea. Now explain why you wanted me here."

"I was set up." Mathias took a long sip of his tea.

"What do you mean?" Lionel set his mug down.

"Do you truly believe I'd be so stupid to reveal my magic in front of a human child?" He was looking at Lionel as he answered. "Not to mention, why would I?"

"I've heard rumors." Lionel picked up his mug again. "Of a group. A group who wants our kind to step out of the shadows."

"You've heard right." Mathias nodded. "And I'm part of that group."

"Then you did what you were accused of." Lionel rolled his shoulders back.

"I did not. Why would I have revealed my magic to a child? It makes no sense. It does nothing to help us achieve our goals."

"But why would someone set you up?" Lionel took another sip of tea. "That makes no sense either."

"Because they want to bring us down. The Elite." Mathias picked up a chocolate biscuit.

"The Elite?" I knew I'd heard that name before, but I couldn't place it. It was like deja vu or something. It felt off.

"Yes. Have you heard of us, Gloria?" Mathias took a small bite of the cookie.

"I'm not sure."

Lionel frowned. "You okay?"

"Yeah. I'm fine." And I was, aside from an uneasy feeling both inside and out.

LIONEL

## Lionel

*T*ruth-seer tea. All of that for a magically brewed tea that had revealing powers. Part of me had actually believed he'd poisoned the tea. I knew that was crazy. Did I really think my father would want to kill Glow and me? The problem was I didn't know him. No matter what Mr. Wayes said, building trust was going to be hard.

Yet Glow seemed to have no trouble with it at all. And that worried me a lot. She was convinced he'd ended her suffering, and maybe he did, but he didn't do it for innocent reasons. Everything he did was selfish, and the last thing I wanted was for her to be in the middle of it.

"It's about to start." Mathias hunched over. He was Mathias. I had to stop viewing him as my father. He was a crazy man, and our only connection was that I had half his genes.

"What's about to start?" Glow had such patience. Maybe it was different for her because she wasn't related to the guy.

"It. The torture."

"Torture?" Crazy or not, Mathias was scared. I hated that there was nothing I could do now to keep Glow away from this.

"Yes." He wrapped his hands around the mug again. "Did you both finish your tea?"

"Yes." Glow looked over at me. There was worry in her eyes.

"Good. You will see all for what it is, and you may have a chance to get out of here with your mind."

"Once again, I ask you, if it's that bad, why did you want me to come?" I felt for the guy despite myself, but he had insisted I come. And I had. And not alone.

"Because you are the only one who might help. And you aren't safe. No one is safe right now."

The lights flickered.

"Get ready." Mathias's teeth chattered. "Get ready now."

The lights flickered again before going out completely. There wasn't a hint of light in the place. I scooted over and took Glow's hand. "We can handle this."

"I know." Her voice was low, but she sounded okay.

"If in doubt, shift. Okay? Don't worry about your

magic; let your wolf take over. She will be your best form of protection."

"If you can shift," Mathias whispered. "I usually can't."

"Bloody hell." Because that was what we needed.

"Will the lights go back on soon?" Glow asked.

"Not until you don't want them to." Mathias voice quivered. I assumed he was shaking.

"Oh, I'll want them to come back on." Glow sounded pretty normal, but she had to be nervous. At least I was. Sitting in a completely dark prison with my crazy father made things more than a little ominous.

"Trust me. You won't." Mathias coughed and then cleared his throat. "Get ready. They are coming."

"Who is coming?" I didn't really want to know, but I had to ask.

There was a screeching sound, akin to nails on a chalkboard.

"Ugh. It's back." Glow groaned. "The taste is back."

"Remember, your mind will always be yours." Mathias sounded closer, and I assumed he was moving around the table to where we sat. "If you can keep them out."

"Okay, Mathias. Enough with the riddles. How do we get out of here?" I knew getting angry wouldn't help, but given the situation, I needed him to get real with us.

"You can't yet."

"Make it stop." Glow groaned again. "Please, make it stop."

"Is it that sound or the taste?"

"It's both. And the smell. Can't you smell that?" There was pain in her voice. Pain I needed to get rid of.

"She's got a powerful magic sense, son." Mathias's voice came from right next to me now. "I don't know what you were thinking bringing her here, but if she can fight this, she can fight anything."

"I wasn't thinking, okay? I'm an idiot." And if something happened to her, I would never forgive myself.

"No. Stop." Glow squeezed my hand. "We've been over this. Please. It's not your fault. I can handle this."

"Can she wield magic the way she can sense it?" Mathias asked.

"Not yet. But she's getting there." Now wasn't the time to push her.

"Don't make this woman mad. You will lose." Mathias laughed. It was a strange sound given his earlier tone and the fact that we were huddled in the darkness.

"I'm not worried about that right now."

"Nor should you be."

The screeching grew louder. There was a flash of light before something cold splashed against me.

"What the hell was that?" I wiped a wet gooey substance off my face.

No one replied.

"Mathias? What the hell was that?" No response. "What was that?"

"Mathias?" Glow grabbed hold of my arm. "What is this stuff?"

I assumed she meant the goo. I was actually kind of

127

grateful it was dark because I had a feeling I didn't want to see what was all over me.

Things went quiet.

"The next one will be sooner. It goes back and forth." Mathias was whispering so low I could barely hear him.

We sat without really moving for a few minutes, and then sure enough, the screeching was back, ear piercing. Gloria groaned. Another spray of something cold and wet splashed across me, this time even more than the first time. Thank God I had my mouth shut, or I would have ingested the crap.

"We have to get out of here." I held tightly onto Glow's hand.

"Not without your dad."

"I know." I did. There was no way I was leaving him with whatever the hell this was. This was inhumane. And even if they were right about him, exposing his true nature to a human didn't mean he deserved this torture.

A horrifying scream pierced the air.

"That's Hyna," Mathias muttered. "Poor Hyna. I don't think she can make it much longer."

"We are getting everyone out of here." Glow's voice sounded stronger. "No one should have to live with this."

"Yes. We will." I'd thought the other area halls we'd moved through had been bad, but this was something else. It was like a twisted carnival ride with a 4D element.

Glow screamed. I looked over to see a grotesque face glowing in front of her. I lunged for it, but the face disappeared.

"Keep your mind yours," Mathias commanded.

"I don't know what that means." And I was getting tired of the riddles. I needed something helpful. Something straightforward.

"It means don't let them win."

"We aren't letting them win." Glow's voice was strained. I could feel the dark magic, but she felt it on a whole different, horrible level.

"How many others are in here? Just those two we passed?" I needed to know what kind of rescue mission we were moving into.

"Now, yes. The others succumbed."

"Succumbed?" I hoped that didn't mean what it sounded like.

"Yes. Lost their minds."

"Okay. Fantastic." I braced myself as another round of screeching started. This time I was ready when the liquid pelted me. "We are getting out. The face will probably appear soon, but everyone stay calm." I had no idea what was going on, but I knew the sooner we got out of this hell hole, the better.

"There's no probably. It will. It always does after the first part of the cycle." Mathias sounded calmer now.

"How do we get out of here?" Glow gasped.

I pulled her into my arms. I hated the pain and suffering she was dealing with.

"I don't know." Mathias sighed. "If I knew, don't you think I would have left already?"

"You have to be kidding me." He didn't even know how to get out? But this wasn't the time to get annoyed and frustrated. "We will have to use magic to break through that door and get out the front."

"They won't let you take me out the front," Mathias stated. "They can't."

"We can't leave you here." Bad relationship or not, he was my father. Not to mention, he was a living being. No one deserved this hell.

"You can. Just find a way to come back and get me. Get someone to help."

"Who?" If there was someone else who could help, then why did he make me come? "Glow?" She hadn't said anything in a while.

"I'm okay. I just threw up, I think. Not on you, I hope."

"You think? You okay, babe? And like I care if it's on me. I'm already covered in this weird shit."

"That smell. That taste. Ugh." She leaned into my chest.

"I know." I didn't know exactly what she was going through, but I could only imagine how bad it was.

"Get her out of here, son." Mathias patted my arm. "Forget about me and the others. This is dangerous."

"They let you take my call. I don't get it. They knew I'd be walking into this?"

"I don't know what they know about this wing. It's not run by the warden."

"Then who is it run by?" None of it made sense.

"I don't know. And whoever it is doesn't expect you to get out."

"What do you mean? The guards said we should get out alive."

"Alive doesn't mean with your mind intact." His words rang true. Alive didn't mean untouched.

"Get out. You can do it. I can hold on for a few more weeks." He pushed against my shoulder.

"I have an idea." Gloria pulled away from me.

"What are you doing, Glow?" I held onto her hand. "We are supposed to stay together."

"Yeah, well, sometimes you have to call an audible in life."

I wanted to yank her back, but I knew I couldn't hold her back. However, I wasn't letting her do this alone. "I'm coming."

"It's too dark. We'll lose each other anyway."

"Not necessarily. Where are you going?"

"To find the source of this magic."

"You think you know where that is?" I wouldn't have been remotely surprised if she did.

"Yes." She sounded farther away. "Stay with Mathias. He's been through this too many times. No one comes in here. If we can destroy the source, we can protect the prisoners, get out, and then come back for them. It's the only thing that's going to work."

She was right about it being the only way, but that didn't mean I was sitting back. "No. We stay together. I'm sorry. We can call some audibles, but not that."

"Fine. But we have to move."

"You set the pace. I promise I'll be with you the whole time." I meant it.

# GLOW

*I* wasn't sure how I knew, but I did. I knew it all went back to the area by the door to enter this wing. It had to have been anchored near the spot where the sensation had been so bad I'd thought I'd choke. If Mathias hadn't blocked things for me, I might have died. That was why I was going back there.

This was inhumane. Beyond inhumane. It was like a mad scientist was running the wing. But I got the distinct impression no one was running it. At least not in a routine, on-site way. This wasn't magic being performed on-site. This was magic set up and left with the goal of destroying these people. Even if it weren't for the taste and smell, I would have been sick.

The tea had helped me, as Mathias had promised. Although the face had scared me, I'd also seen that was all it was—a face. There was no body. No menacing hands. It was a face that may not have even really been there. The tea stopped me from imagining more than what was really there.

And that was what Mathias must have meant. So much of this was in our head. It made me wonder if we were even really wet. I ran a hand down my shirt. Yes. We were wet. I couldn't be imaging that disgusting gel-like stuff. I wished I weren't really tasting, smelling, and feeling the magic, but that wasn't supposed to happen. The goal was to make you feel like you were going crazy, to doubt yourself.

The feeling of doubt over my own thoughts and memories wasn't a new one. I'd felt that way late first semester. I'd had all sorts of strange dreams that made no sense. And then, I'd see kids on campus and feel like I knew them, only to realize I'd met them in a dream.

That was all caused by stress; this was man-made or, more specifically, magic made. Different, but at its core, not that different in the way it affected your mind and sense of reality.

We neared the doors, and I fought the urge to vomit again. There was nothing left in me but bile, and I couldn't add that burning sensation to the pain I was already dealing with.

The screeching started again. The gross liquid. The face. It was endless. Like one big loop, although the intervals were off a little.

"You okay, Glow?" Lionel asked after the face disappeared.

"Yes. I'm okay." Even if I wasn't okay, I wouldn't have

told him. We had to push through. We had no other choice.

We made it to the doors, and I knew we didn't have long before the cycle started again. We were due for another quick turnaround. Maybe it wasn't a perfect interval, but there was some sort of pattern. "It has to be around here."

"You think it's an object?" Lionel seemed to have figured out the same thing I did.

"What else could it be?"

"It could be almost anything... this level of magic."

"I know. But let's hope it's something obvious."

"That's quite a big thing to ask for."

It was too dark to see anything, but we kept searching.

"Wait a second." A thought struck me out of nowhere like a bolt of lightning. "Do you have the key they gave you?"

"Yeah, but I looked when we first got in. There's no keyhole on this side."

"I know, but I need to see it."

He handed me the key. The metallic taste got so bad I doubled over.

"Glow!" Lionel's arms came around my waist.

"This key opens more than the doors." I forced myself to focus on the key, even though it was making everything worse.

Before I could say more, the screeching started again. I waited for the gel to pummel us and the face to appear. Finally, it stopped. "This opens something else."

"This is impossible to see in the dark." He sighed. "I tried to get a light to start before, but I couldn't. I don't know why this place has blocked my magic."

"I'm sure there's a spell doing it."

"But... it can't stop mine since I don't have mine yet." A thought hit me. "So if I can pull mine out fast enough, maybe I can get us out."

"How do you figure?" He found my hand and squeezed it. "I'm not saying I don't agree, but I am not following."

"The spell is blocking you from using magic, but it can't block me since I don't even know how to use it."

"So? How can it help you if you can't use it?"

"No spell is perfect. Right? They taught us that in Magic Theory first semester."

"Right."

"So there has to be a work-around. You can't find it because you already know how you like to use magic. It comes naturally. But if I can find a way to bring mine out that works under these conditions..."

"Glow, that's a great idea and all, but you know how hard getting your magic out is under ideal conditions. These are not ideal." He didn't need to say more.

"Well, do you have any other ideas?" I asked. "Because I don't plan to lose my mind in here. I have too much to do outside of here."

"We aren't losing our minds in here. I won't let it happen."

"Then help me." I knew that ultimately getting my magic out was on me.

"You know I'll help you with anything you need. "

I did know. "Okay."

The screeching started again. I couldn't take anymore. I closed my eyes and tried to block it out. I tried to picture the sound… what it would look like. I could see the sound waves. The ups and downs. And then I pictured cutting up the waves. The sound stopped. I opened my eyes.

"That stopped early." Lionel had some excitement in his voice. "Did you do something?"

"I don't know. Shouldn't that liquid have hit us already?"

"Yes. And the mask!" He was beyond excited now. "You stopped it."

"Hey, we don't know that. It might be a pause. And maybe it wasn't even me. I just pictured destroying the sound waves."

"You just pictured it?" There was awe in his voice. "You're incredible, Glow."

"I'm not incredible."

"Try something."

"Okay. What?" I was game to try anything if it was going to help us. I felt so much better now. Not only had the torture stopped, but the metallic taste had subsided. It was still there, but not overwhelming. That was for sure.

"You know how you pictured the sound waves?"

"Yeah?" I wondered where he was going with this.

"Try to picture the lights somehow. Picture whatever is keeping them off, and make them turn back on."

"Oh." I hadn't thought about that. "I'll try." I closed

my eyes and pictured the spells keeping the lights off. I pictured destroying the spells the same way I pictured the sound waves.

The lights flooded the hall. I blinked, trying to get used to the light.

"Was it her?" Mathias walked toward us.

"It was."

"It's here." I walked over to a space above the door. "Here, help me." I pointed up to a cabinet above the door.

Lionel gave me a boost, and I inserted the key. I pulled out what appeared to be a burnt piece of rope.

Lionel gently placed me back on the ground.

"You destroyed an item of dark magic." Mathias walked over and held out his hand. "Can I see it?"

I didn't see any reason not to let him see it. I handed it over.

"Thank you. You two need to leave. Now. Before anyone notices the change. And send help."

"We still have to find a way out of here."

"Wait." Lionel looked at his watch. "It's almost four. Visiting hours are almost over. They made a huge deal out of that. Maybe they'll come back and get us."

"You think?" That would be an amazing outcome, but I doubted it.

"Only one way to find out." Lionel started to pound on the door.

Nothing happened at first, then there was the sound of metal clanging like the lock was falling away. The door creaked open a tiny crack.

"Are you sure we shouldn't try to get them out today?" I asked Lionel.

"It's not worth the risk of them going after you. Leave and send help," Mathias breathed.

"Okay." Lionel shook his father's hand. "We will get you out."

I shook his hand next. "I promise. We won't leave you here."

"You've already done so much." He kissed my hand. "Thank you."

He released my hand, and Lionel slipped his hand into the tiny crack in the door. We slipped out. As soon as we reached the other side, a guard, dressed in what looked an awful lot like a hazmat suit, slammed the door shut behind us and locked it.

I didn't quite believe Mathias wasn't trying to come out. Was he that afraid we'd get in some sort of trouble? Fathers, even estranged ones, had done stranger things for their children.

The hell hall didn't seem so bad this time. I knew how to handle the taste now. I pushed it away. I ignored the catcalls and taunts, and we finally reached the front. While I waited for the guard to get our stuff, I at last said what was on my mind. "Can you believe we did that?"

"No. Not at all. But that wasn't we. That was all you." Lionel put an arm around me. "You did that."

I finally looked at Lionel. Really looked at him. I looked at the pink goo all over him. I looked down. I had it all over me too. We also had dirt and dust sticking to it. "Oh my gosh, we're disgusting."

"We are. But we're alive. We have our minds. We left my dad in better shape. And you wielded magic." He spoke at the lowest whisper possible, but it didn't seem necessary. The guard was wearing headphones and didn't seem particularly interested in us.

"I wielded magic." Now that we were in the entry-way, the panic and adrenaline had faded enough to let that reality sink in. I had wielded my magic in a seriously cool way.

"Did you find your father?" The guard from when we entered came out holding my bag and Lionel's phone.

"Yes." Lionel nodded.

"What's all that stuff?" He pointed at the pink goo.

"We're not sure," I answered honestly.

"Okay. Well, hope we don't see you back here for a while." Gary handed over our stuff and opened the front door.

"We hope to never see you again either." I eagerly stepped back outside. I sucked in the fresh air as we hurried over to the SUV.

Lionel pointed up. "Those clouds look ominous."

"Nothing can be as ominous as what we just went through."

"True." He held open my door.

I couldn't relax until the gates opened, and we drove back onto the highway. "That really was insane."

"That's putting it mildly."

"We need to get to Mr. Wayes. He's the only one I know we can trust."

"Or we hope we can trust."

"If we can't trust him, we have nowhere else to turn."
I rested my head on his shoulder.

"You're right."

The rain started before we even made it to the inter-state. It was the kind of rain that made it nearly impos-sible to see. The few cars on the road had pulled over.

"There's a sign for a motel. Should we see if they have a room?" I assumed he wouldn't read into my suggesting of getting a room together, but I wasn't about to stay alone. I didn't even want to think about the night-mares that were probably waiting for me.

# LIONEL

"One room please." I didn't say anything as Glow answered the clerk's questions. The last thing I wanted to do was get separate rooms, but I wasn't about to be the one to suggest it.

"How do you want to pay? Cash or credit?" the clerk asked.

"Credit." I slid my card across the counter. There was no way I was letting her pay, considering we were only stuck there because we'd visited my father. Not to mention the hell I'd just put her through because she kept me company.

The clerk ran the card and then slid both my credit card and a room key across the counter. "You are in room twelve. Have a good night."

"Thanks." I took both cards and walked to the door. Glow followed, and we made our way down the outside hallway to room twelve.

I unlocked the door. The room was nicer than I expected, but I don't think either of us cared at all.

"I know we should probably shower, but what's the point?" Glow sat down on the edge of the bed. "We have nothing to change into."

"You can still shower if you want."

"Oh, I know. Maybe I'll just rinse off really quick and sleep in a towel."

"That's fine. And I can sleep on the floor."

She wrinkled her nose. "Are you serious? Sleep on that floor?"

"Okay. I'd rather not, but whatever you need."

"We were talking about how convenient it was that we lived on the same floor the other day." She kicked off her boots. "Somehow, I think we can share a bed tonight."

"Well, I'm all about it if you are. I just don't want you to feel like we have to. I know it's been a crazy day."

"That's even more of a reason to share a bed. Do you think I want to be alone at all?"

"I have to agree with you there." I took off my boots and pulled off my disgusting shirt. I knew I'd have no desire to put it back on in the morning. But I would worry about that in the morning.

"We should probably get food."

"Want me to go to vending machines?"

"Sure. I need to shower." She stood up. Her eyes went to my bare chest, and they widened a little. "Could you get me something chocolate. I need chocolate."

"Any particular type of chocolate?"

"Anything. But if it has peanut butter, it's even better."

I laughed. "Okay. I'll see what I can find."

I hated leaving her alone, but I knew she was fine. She was more than fine. She had just gone from regular badass to queen of the badasses in my mind.

I headed back down toward the office where I'd seen the machines. I picked out a variety of candy, careful to get a few things with peanut butter, as well as some crackers and pretzels to add in something marginally healthy.

The shower was running when I got back to the room. I sat down and finally checked my phone. I had texts from Terrance and Keeton. I ignored both. What could I tell them? It was not like they'd even believe me if I tried to explain to them what we'd just been through.

The water turned off, and a few minutes later the bathroom door opened. She walked out with a small white towel wrapped around her. Her long hair was wet where it fell down her back. My body responded immediately, and I knew it was going to be a hard night—no pun intended. "Hey, any luck at the machines?"

"See for yourself." I pointed to where I'd dropped the pile of food.

"Nice. Want me to wait for you to shower?" She eyed the candy.

"No. Go ahead. I won't be long."

"You sure?"

I could tell she was hungry. I most certainly didn't

want her to wait. "Oh, yes, because this meal is so formal we can't possibly eat it separately."

She laughed. "Okay. Good point. Have a good shower. The water is nice and hot."

"Thanks." I headed into the bathroom and closed the door. I debated whether to take a hot shower or a cold one. I needed the cold one to deal with my thoughts about Glow; I needed the hot one to wash off the day. I went with hot. At least the Glow thoughts were good ones.

I followed her lead and left my dirty clothes in the bathroom and headed out in just a towel. Mine around my waist.

"Hey." She was under the sheets already. "I saved you a few things."

"That was awfully generous of you." I grabbed a pack of candy and slid into the other side of the bed.

"It was, wasn't it?" She reached for a bag of pretzels. I was glad I'd gone with a few non-candy options.

"Very." I opened the candy. "Especially after you saved us today."

"Hey, you weren't so shabby either."

"But you were the one who got that crazy torture stuff to stop."

"I was, wasn't I?" She put the empty pretzel bag down on the bedside and slipped down more in the bed. "What a crazy day."

"Crazy doesn't quite cover it. I don't know what word does." I put my wrapper down and rolled over onto my side.

"Well, if I had to go through such a horrible experience, I'm glad I did it with you. There is no one else I would have wanted by my side." She rolled onto her side as well.

It was only a double bed. I hadn't really thought about how small that would be until we'd both rolled over and were quite close together. "I wouldn't have wanted to go through that with anyone else either."

"Romantic, right?"

I laughed. "So romantic. At least we had our first date at Last Call."

"Well, we didn't end up in bed after that one."

"True. We are in bed now." In bed wearing nothing but towels. I couldn't help but picture how easy it would be to remove the towels and explore one another's bodies.

"You don't have to stay so far away from me." She reached out a hand toward me.

"Is that your way of asking me to get closer?"

"Yes."

She didn't have to ask me twice. I moved over, resting my head on the same pillow with her.

"You're so beautiful." I looked into her brown eyes.

"Thank you."

"Can I kiss you?"

"Do you really need to ask? We've kissed before."

"Yeah. But not wearing only towels in bed."

"No, I guess not. But I was on your lap."

"You were." The combination of talking about her on my lap and knowing how quickly I could have her naked was about to kill me. I couldn't wait a second more. I pressed a gentle kiss to her lips. Then quickly I turned it into something entirely non-gentle. I made the kiss hard, demanding. I bit down on her lip, knowing she liked it as much as I did. I liked that I was getting to know her desires. I needed to know more of them. All of them.

The kiss intensified and she moved on top of me, offsetting the towel in the process. My hands found her breasts while my lips slid down her neck. She tasted so good. She felt so good.

She pulled my towel off from around my waist and took me in her hand. Her hand felt so good as she stroked me.

"I want you, Lionel. I know this thing with us is new, but I don't want to wait."

"No one said we had to wait." I wouldn't push her into anything, but that didn't mean I was going to slow things down either.

"Good." She kissed my neck and then started to kiss down my body. I closed my eyes and enjoyed the sensation of her lips on me until I couldn't wait anymore. I rolled her over and moved above her. I slipped my hand between her legs, loving the moans and panting it created. "I need you, Lionel."

"I need you." I moved my fingers and thrust into her. Within seconds, I knew I was where I was always meant to be.

Sex wasn't supposed to be that good. At least no sex

I'd had had ever been like that. And now that I'd experienced this level of connection, I knew I'd never settle for anything less.

Glow stirred beside me, and I pressed a kiss to her forehead. She opened her eyes. "Hey."

"Good morning, beautiful."

"Is it really morning already?" She yawned. It was a fair question, as the room was still dark.

"It is." I wasn't happy about it either, but the clock matched the time on my phone. "It's after ten already."

"After ten?" Her eyes widened. "We slept that long?"

"Well, we didn't do all that much sleeping." I grinned. "I mean we did have sex four times..."

"We did, didn't we?" She reached for me, wrapping her arms around my neck. She pulled me down on top of her. "I promise I'm not starting anything. I know we need to get moving back to campus, but I need a few more kisses before then."

"You can have as many kisses as you want." I ran my lips down her neck. My lips kept going there. My wolf was already begging to mate with her, but I knew it wasn't time yet.

"Okay. I can't handle this. I'm already turned on. We should stop." She pushed against me.

I laughed but moved off her. "You act like it's a bad thing that you're turned on. Or that it's just you that's turned on."

"Wait. You are too?" She reached her hand down. "Yes, you are." She grinned. "Do you think we have a few minutes?"

"We already slept till ten. What's another half hour?" I brushed my lips against hers.

"Half hour?" She put her hands on either side of my face.

"Yes. I need at least that long to properly enjoy you."

"Uh-oh. You've got that look in your eye." Her eyes lit up.

"What look?"

"The naughty one. The one where I know I'm about to experience something earth-shatteringly good."

"I want you to experience that every time." I slid my hand between her legs, and made it my mission to remind her of how hot things were with us.

\* \* \*

IT WAS after lunchtime by the time we'd left the motel, stopped for breakfast at Waffle House, and made our way back toward campus.

"So that was interesting." She was grinning. She was also glowing.

I was proud of myself.

"Amazing. Interesting. Whatever you want to call it."

"Both."

"Yes. Both." I took her hand.

"But I guess we should focus now. I don't want to wait too long before we talk to Mr. Wayes. We can't leave your father and the others waiting around."

"Agreed." I put my arm around the back of her seat. "I feel bad enough we left."

"Me too. And we just spent last night..."

"Yeah, I know. But we had to spend the night there anyway, so we just used our time well."

"That is true." She said the words, but it didn't sound like she believed them.

"Hey." I ran my fingers down her cheek. "We did nothing wrong. After what we went through..."

"It was amazing though. I mean the stuff with us. Right?" She looked over at me.

"It was beyond amazing. I never knew that level of connection was possible."

"We barely know each other..."

"Sure we do. We've lived in the same dorm for months."

"Yeah, but how often had we talked?"

"I think after what we happened at the prison we've experienced plenty together."

She leaned into my hand. "So I guess we're officially a couple now?"

"Of course. I'm not going anywhere." I hated to see her look so nervous.

"Good." She sighed. "We talk to Mr. Wayes, get the prisoners out, and then we can focus on us."

"Sounds like a perfect plan." Even though, I'd be focusing on us the whole time anyway.

We talked about everything and nothing the rest of the way back. I learned a whole lot more about her food preferences and her childhood pets. She learned about my love of football and tacos. Very important topics.

It was late afternoon by the time I parked in front of

Convenience. We didn't waste time and headed right inside.

Mr. Wayes was in front of the counter talking to a woman I'd never seen before.

Glow marched right up to them, pulling me along with her. "We need to talk to you."

"Yes." Mr. Wayes looked us over. We were, of course, back in our pink goo-covered clothing. "I can see that."

"Alone." Glow tapped her foot. "I'm sorry."

"Nina can be with us." Mr. Wayes pointed at the woman. "I assure you, she's trustworthy."

"No." I shook my head. "She can't. I'm sorry. I don't know who she is, and this is a big deal." We had no idea who was in on the prison. I knew we were taking a chance even talking to Mr. Wayes. But my father and Glow both felt that we should trust him, and he was the only hope we had.

"It's fine, Adam. We can talk later." The woman patted his shoulder before heading out through the front door.

"I wasn't lying. Nina is trustworthy." He looked at the door she'd just walked through.

"This is huge, Mr. Wayes." Glow leaned back against the counter.

"I believe you." He was staring at our clothing again.

"This." She gestured to her shirt. "Is only part of it."

"I take it you visited Lionel's father..." He rubbed the stubble on his chin. I had my share of stubble now too, but shaving wasn't high on my list at the moment. I did need to find out what Glow thought of beards. This was the time of year when I usually grew one.

"How'd you guess?" Glow yawned.

We'd gotten some sleep the night before, but she was still running on such a deficit.

Mr. Wayes raised an eyebrow. "I'd hope you didn't get that way on campus."

"Did you know what you were sending us into?" I had to know. Did he realize how bad it was really going to be?

"No." He shook his head. "I did not. I still don't know. But I'm ready for you to tell me."

"Good. Because if you let me bring Glow into—" I stopped myself. What was done was done.

Evidently, I didn't stop myself before it annoyed Glow. "Stop, okay? We went over this like a thousand times. You didn't bring me into anything. I chose to go. Plus, in the end, it was good I was there."

"It was." I leaned back against the counter next to her.

"You used your magic." Mr. Wayes moved behind the desk and carried out a chair.

"I did." Glow smiled.

"She was amazing," I added. "Absolutely, positively amazing."

Mr. Wayes took a seat. "I have no doubt she was."

"And she can taste magic. Smell it." I wondered if Glow understood the full significance of what she could do.

"That was not amazing. It was horrible." She put a hand to her throat.

"Dark magic..." He looked off into the distance.

"Of course." Glow started to play with the purple ends of her hair again. It was obviously a habit of hers.

Mr. Wayes returned his attention to us. "What kind of dark magic are we talking about?"

"Bad. We are talking torture bad." I started in on the story, and Glow added details as we went. It was crazy telling the story to someone else. I felt like a raving lunatic detailing the cycle of screeching, the liquid goo, the face.

"So it was a track. A track of magic." Mr. Wayes rubbed his chin again.

"Yes. But it was bad. I can absolutely see how it would drive someone mad." It would have driven me mad if I'd been stuck there much longer.

"Oh, I have no doubt. The only question is, who set it up? I struggle to believe the wardens know it's going on." He rested an elbow on his leg.

"Exactly." Glow straightened up. "But you can do something, right?"

Mr. Wayes nodded. "I will make some calls, but are you two all right?"

"Define all right." Glow put a hand in her jean pocket. "Traumatized a bit. But we are physically okay. I'm never going back though. Well, unless I can't get my magic to work somewhere else. I'll go back if that's the only way I can use it."

"I'm sure that's not the case. Have at it in the back."

"Now?" Her brows knit together.

"Is there somewhere else you need to be?"

She looked down. "I probably should change."

"Then make your practice fast, but you should reassure yourself you can do it when your life isn't in danger."

"Any interest in staying around with me?" She looked at me.

"Always." I linked my arm with hers and headed toward the back room.

"What the hell happened to you?" Penny's jaw fell open when I walked into the room.

"It's a long story." I yawned. "It's really late." I had gotten my magic to work fairly quickly. The problem was once I started, I didn't want to stop. Then Mr. Wayes insisted we eat dinner. So it was already after ten o'clock when I made it back to my room.

"Then start talking." She gestured wildly with her hands.

"After my shower." I pulled my towel off the hook and grabbed my toiletries. "I am too gross to wait a second more."

"Come on. You can't leave me hanging." She wrung her hands at her side.

"Yes, I can. I'm disgusting." Sure I'd showered the night before, but I'd put back on the gross clothes. I never did find out what that pink goo was, and I didn't want to know. These clothes were going in the trash once I got them off. Thankfully, I'd worn my oldest jeans. And pink goo aside, I needed to get cleaned up anyway. I'd had sex five times. Sex was great and all, but it also was the kind of thing you are supposed to shower after. I opened the door and started down the hall.

"Hey, Glow. Come on." Penny followed me right into the communal bath.

"Give me ten minutes. It's not going to take me long." I turned on the water in one of the stalls. The nice thing about the late hour was that I didn't have to wait on anyone to find a free stall.

"Bull. You don't take ten-minute showers." Penny tightened the tie on her terry-cloth robe.

"No. Generally, I don't." I took rather long ones. "But I'll make an exception this time and get myself moving."

"I'm going to stand right out here and wait." She stamped her foot.

"Are you serious?" I was sure she had better things to do than stand around the bathroom. Plus, she was being ridiculous. It was perfectly normal to want to shower before chatting.

"Otherwise, you'll be in there an hour."

"There isn't enough hot water for me to take an hour shower." I wasn't that rude, no matter how much I loved a good, long shower.

"I'll just wait, then."

"Suit yourself." I closed the curtain. I was too tired to

argue with her. I washed my body, trying to rinse away all the memories of the prison while holding on to the amazing memories from my night with Lionel. How had I experienced two such polar opposite experiences in a single day? Maybe that was the point. One was so bad that we needed something equally good. I washed my hair then reluctantly turned off the shower. I wrapped myself in my towel and opened the curtain. I came face-to-face with Penny. She hadn't been kidding about waiting for me.

I slipped into my favorite old PJs, the kind where the pants had holes and I really didn't care. I lay back on my bed. "Okay. What do you want to know?"

She took a seat on her desk chair. "What happened? All you said was some weird stuff about a road trip with Lionel. You disappeared and you came back looking like hell."

"I did."

"So what happened?" Her voice dripped with impatience.

"Uh, Lionel and I are a couple now."

"Wait. What?" She shot out of her chair. "How does that explain anything?"

"Isn't that really what you want to know?" She'd seemed excited about us getting together before I left.

"That's great and all... but why did you look so crazy?"

"You know, crazy night." I didn't want to tell Penny about the prison. I didn't want to tell anyone else about it.

It was such a messed up experience that I wanted to put it behind me forever.

"Crazy night? Next, you are going to tell me you slept with Lionel.."

"I did."

"Wait. What?" Penny blanched. "Slept with meaning sex?"

"Yes." I grinned. I could feel my whole face flush.

"And you're grinning."

"Yes, I am." I had nothing to be embarrassed about.

"So it was good, then?" She sat back down in her chair.

"Amazing." I closed my eyes and imagined looking up at him.

"But why did you look like you fell down a well?"

Her voice pulled me from my fantasy. I opened my eyes. "Uh, that's a not so fun story."

"Tell me."

"I'd rather not." The more she pushed, the less I wanted to tell.

"Why not?" she pressed. "Why do you need to have secrets from me?"

"It's not about having secrets. I told you about the sex." I'd shared the juicy details. The rest wasn't a fun story.

"Then what is it?"

"It's upsetting to talk about. I'd rather not." I slipped under my covers. I still needed to get up and brush my teeth, but I might as well get comfortable. "But I can let you in on another secret."

"Fine, but that doesn't mean I'm not going to drop the other." Penny could be bossy, but this was something else. Something had to have been bothering her, but I didn't even have the energy to question her about it. That would have to wait for morning.

"This one will more than make up for it." At least I thought it would, but considering how little she cared about my sex life who even knew anymore.

"I admit the sex thing was good. Is this better?" She pulled her chair over to sit by my bed. That was a bit odd.

"I guess it depends how you define better."

"Just spit it out." She pulled her legs up under her so she was sitting cross-legged.

"I used magic."

"Wait. what?" Her eyes widened.

"Yes!" I waited for her to start getting excited. This was the part of things I wanted to talk about.

"Are you for real? Not just the feeling stuff you've been doing?" Her voice was cold.

"Yeah... for real. Why aren't you more excited? I won't have to leave the academy."

"You wouldn't have had to leave anyway. I was going to make sure of it. I have your back."

"Thanks, but I couldn't stay past this year if I couldn't use magic. You can't be in a hybrid house if you aren't a real hybrid." And it felt so good not to have to worry about that anymore.

"But you are." She stood up and knelt beside the bed. She put a hand on my shoulder. "You've always been one, whether you can use magic or not." She squeezed my shoulder so hard it kind of hurt. "You don't need to stress about any of this."

"I'm not stressing. Well, I wasn't. But now you are freaking me out. Why do I get the sense you aren't happy for me?" Had I inadvertently pissed her off? No. I pushed away the thought. I'd done nothing wrong. This was her issue. I was all about taking responsibility when I messed up, but I'd been a pretty darn good roommate given the circumstances.

"I'm happy if you aren't pushing yourself too hard." She returned to her chair. "You have to take things slow."

"Slow?" She had to be kidding. "I'm almost nineteen."

"You know what I mean. It's still early in the semester."

"So what?"

"So, don't push yourself so hard you get hurt." She crossed her arms over her chest.

"I really don't understand why you can't be happy for me." Was this what it was? She liked being friends with me when I was incapable and helpless. Now that I was going to be on an equal playing field, she didn't want me around or something?

"I'm so happy for you." She put on an obviously fake smile. She wasn't even trying. "I'm just tired. It's late."

"Yeah. It's very late." I grabbed my toothbrush and toothpaste. "I need to brush my teeth." I headed down the hall, hoping she wouldn't follow. I searched my reflection in the mirror as I brushed. Shouldn't something have looked different?

She was in her bed, facing the wall when I returned.

Relief hit me. I couldn't take any more conflict until I got some sleep. I slipped into bed and turned off the light. Finally. My bed. The only thing that would have made it better would have been to have Lionel with me.

I slipped into uneasy dreams right away.

*I was right outside a dorm room. It wasn't Wolf Bound. I could tell by the red tie hanging over the back of the chair. This was a Wolf Blood's dorm.*

*There were people lying there on the floor, and I was blowing something into the room. Pixie dust or something. The green dust seeped into their pores, nose, and down their throats.*

*"It's done," I said to someone I couldn't see. "They won't remember a thing to do with the Elite now."*

I woke up in a sweat. The Elite? Wasn't that what Mathias had talked about? Something about the dream nagged at me. It was another of those that felt so eerily real. But there was nothing to be done about that now. I rolled back over, ready to go to sleep.

I had fallen back to sleep, into dreams I didn't remember, when I felt a choking sensation. My eyes flew open as I struggled to breathe. There was someone on top of me. Someone with their hands around my neck. Even with the lights off, I could tell who it was—Penny.

"You couldn't just keep things easy? You had to go and mess it all up." She squeezed harder.

I wanted to say something, or to push her away, but I couldn't. I wasn't getting enough oxygen to access my magic.

"You're not the only one with problems. I have problems. Real problems. I have a warlock dad who hates my hybrid mom. He's jealous. I know. He wishes he had a wolf. I can't give him that, but I can give him other help. I can help him take down the hybrids."

I tried to talk again. She seemed to notice it and loosened her hold on my throat. I wanted to push her off, but I knew I should be careful.

"But you're a hybrid," I choked out.

"Yes? So? Wouldn't it be easier to just be one? A wolf or a witch?"

"But that's not who we are." What the hell was going on with her? Normally, she was so proud of her dual nature.

"But he's right about one thing. My father." She made no move to get off me. Her hands were still around my neck, just not squeezing.

"What's that?"

"If the Elite get their way and we come out of the shadows, nothing will ever be the same again. Wolves already think they are superior. That's why we had to set them up. If the powers that be saw how bad the Elite was, they'd destroy it before it could cause any change."

"Set who up?" I needed to get her off me, but I also wanted to keep her talking.

"The hybrids. Like Lionel's dad."

"Wait. What?" I thought of the prison. The magic keeping them there. "That was you? You got him put in there?"

She smiled. "Not me. But my father. Quite elaborate,

isn't it? I know that's where you were. I know you were at the prison."

"You're crazy."

"Not as crazy as you." She smirked. "Starting to remember things, are you?"

"The green dust." I thought about the dream. "You did that."

"Of course I did. I couldn't let those bloods mess things up. It was bad enough when the borns were being recruited. The more students get involved with the Elite the greater the threat becomes. It needs to disappear, and it needs to disappear fast. And what was the best way to do that? From inside. The Elite never expected a thing. They thought wiping the bloods' memories was to protect the organization, instead it was to make sure we could snuff it out without a trace." Her eyes were wild. Who was this girl? Was she really the same Penny?

"You've lost your mind." I struggled to come up with a plan. "And how didn't I know what was going on?"

"I controlled you through your dreams." There was pride in her voice and excitement in her eyes. "It was so easy when you weren't using your magic."

"You're horrible." And I thought she wanted to be my friend. I couldn't imagine a worse violation.

"What did it hurt you? You didn't even know until you worked on getting your magic. Why couldn't you have just focused on your wolf? Everything would have been fine."

"Could you please get off me? Then we can talk." Please? I was still being polite? I was unbelievable.

"I can't. Not now that you know." Tears streamed down her face.

"Sure you can. We can work through this."

"We can't." Her hands returned to my neck and she squeezed.

My vision started to fade and my wolf howled. I was too weak to reach for magic, but my wolf had the strength to save me. I reached for her, letting her take over. I felt the power surge through me as I shifted.

I had the element of surprise, and moments later, I had her on the floor, our positions reversed.

The door flew open. I looked over through my wolf's eyes and saw Lionel with his roommate, Terrance. "Glow?" Lionel stepped inside. "What's going on?"

I growled and pressed my nose into Penny's chest.

"I told you something bad was happening, man." Terrance walked in to stand next to Lionel.

"And I told you, I knew she could take care of herself."

My wolf howled with pride.

"I'M TELLING YOU, I'm innocent." Penny railed as the shifter officers pulled her out of our room.

"Did you or did you not use a spell to physically control a student?" Professor Tyler asked.

"You can't prove it."

"Yes, I can. I can go back and see every spell you've

used. But it will be painful. Are you sure you want me to start that process?"

"Fine. I did it. But it didn't hurt anyone." Penny glared at me. "She didn't even know."

"That's enough." Mr. Wayes walked into the room. "Save it for your attorney."

"She gets an attorney?" Lionel asked. "My dad didn't get one."

"He should have." Mr. Wayes frowned. "And I will be joining the oversight board to make sure that everyone now gets one."

I said nothing. I just watched. I'd changed back into my human form, frustrated that I'd destroyed my favorite pajamas when I shifted, but very much relieved to be alive.

Lionel put an arm around me as Penny was led out of the room.

"If you need me, you know where to find me." Mr. Wayes bowed his head before following the others out and closing the door behind him. Terrance had already left, so Lionel and I were left alone.

"You doing okay?" Lionel tilted my chin so I was looking up at him.

"Sure. I mean it was only two life-threatening experiences in the span of two days, right?" My adrenaline was still running high, but I knew it was only a matter of time before it wore off.

"But there was one good experience in the middle, right?" He waggled his eyebrows.

"Absolutely."

"Want a repeat of that too?"

"Do you really have to ask that question?" I reached up and wrapped my arms around his neck. After the night I'd just had, a little bit of Lionel time was exactly what I needed.

## LIONEL

# Two Months Later

"We have made our decision." Professor Tyler stood up from his spot at the head of the table. The large hall was usually full of students, but today it was just us and a table full of professors dressed in their formal robes.

"No matter what they say, it's going to be okay." Glow squeezed my hand. As always, that touch gave me all the comfort I needed.

"I know." I squeezed her hand back before looking right at the professor and waiting. Glow was right. We would be okay. One of the good parts of our prison experience was I now knew how much we could face, as long as we faced it together.

Professor Tyler cleared his throat. "In light of the

charges being dropped against your father, you are now free to practice magic in any way you choose."

I nodded. "Thank you. I am glad to hear of your decision."

"I am not finished." Professor Tyler frowned.

"Oh, please continue." Patience wasn't exactly my strongest point.

"Now to address the other issue at hand. Your contention that the prohibition against you using magic was unfair and out of line with academy policy."

"Yes." I'd known they would have to lift the prohibition against me, but I had no idea where they'd go on this matter. Glow and I had felt strongly about pushing the administration to examine their policies, and I hoped our effort had paid off. I resisted the urge to loosen my tie. I was hot all of a sudden as we waited.

Professor Tyler made eye contact with each of the other professors at the table before turning back to face us. "We believe you are correct. However, given the current climate on campus, we needed to be extra careful."

By climate he meant the growing concern over the Elite, and the fear of a war brewing. At least that was what I assumed he meant. "Very well."

"And next, we take the matter of Ms. Mayer staying in Wolf Bound." Professor Tyler locked eyes with her.

Glow nodded.

Her jaw was set, but otherwise she seemed calm as she waited.

"Given her impressively fast mastery of magic, we

believe she should stay in Wolf Bound and remain with her class rather than retake her first year."

Glow grinned. "Thank you." We'd been nearly certain she'd be allowed to stay, but retaking first year was a possibility.

"And unless there are other questions, then we will adjourn this special counsel." Professor Tyler returned to his spot behind the head chair.

"Yes, sir." I nodded. There were so many other things I wanted to say, but I didn't want to get us in trouble now that our probation was finally over. Instead, I tightened my hand around Glow's and we walked out through the tall wooden doors and exited onto the quad.

The sun had started to set while we were inside, and the sky was now a gorgeous mix of oranges and pinks.

She stopped midway across the quad. "Well, we didn't change all the rules."

"But we made the administration think about their policies," I pointed out. "That has to count for something." Really, I was so elated we were both out of trouble and staying in the same class together. I knew Glow would be okay if she got held back a year, but selfishly I wanted her to stay in the same year. I wanted us to remain on the same floor the next three years.

"And we got your father and the others out of prison." Her expression darkened for a moment, and I knew she was thinking back on that awful day. I wished we could forget it, but I knew we never would. At least the day had ended with an amazing night neither of us ever wanted to forget. "I still can't believe they were keeping innocent people there because of dark magic from the pure warlocks."

"I can believe it." There was so much evil in the world. But then again, there was also so much beauty. Like the beauty in Glow. "Hey, Glow?"

"Yeah?" Her neck was craned so she could look up at the sky.

I matched her gaze, watching as the darkness took over little by little. "I was meaning to ask you something."

"Ask away." She pulled her eyes from the sky to look at me.

"Want to come home with me for spring break?" I decided to go ahead and ask. "You've already met my father, but I'd love if you met my mother." It was still incredibly strange she knew Mathias yet not the woman who'd raised me.

"Sure, but only if you agree to do a road trip up to Pennsylvania with me this summer and meet my parents and grandmother."

"Absolutely." She wanted me to meet her family? That was a really good sign. "Will your grandmother give us truth-seer tea?"

"Maybe. Does that bother you?" She swung our arms.

"No. I'm okay seeing things for what they are." I stopped short. "I'm okay seeing and doing anything as long as it's with you."

She smiled. "Me too."

"I love you, Glow." I brushed my lips against hers.

"You know I love you too." She rested her head on my chest.

"So what do you want to do now that neither of us are being kicked out?"

"Anything that doesn't involve a trip to a prison." She shivered.

I put my hands on her hips. "How about we get ready for the group run tonight? It is a full moon." There were some really great things about being a wolf, and my wolf was much happier now that he also got to run with Glow's wolf.

"Sure. But until then, there is something else I'd like to do." She grinned and her eyes gleamed.

"What?"

"This." She pressed her lips against mine, and I pulled her into my arms. My second semester of my first year at the Lunar Academy was turning out way better than expected.

# THANK YOU

Thank you for reading *Wolf Bound*. We hope you enjoyed it! Please consider leaving an honest review at your point of purchase. Reviews help us in so many ways!

**Stay up to date with the authors:**

**Visit Alyssa at** https://www.alyssaroseivy.com

**Stay up to date on Alyssa's new releases**: ARI New Release Newsletter.

**To see a complete list of Alyssa's books, please visit**: http://www.alyssaroseivy.com/book-list-faq/

**Visit Jennifer at** https://jennifersnyderbooks.com

**Stay up to date on Jennifer's new releases:** Jennifer's Newsletter

**To see a complete list of Jennifer's books please visit:** https://jennifersnyderbooks.com/book-list/

**The Lunar Academy continues with Wolf Bitten, Year One.**

# WANT MORE LUNAR ACADEMY?

Eager to find out more? The Lunar Academy continues in Wolf Bitten, book four in year one. New House. New Couple. New Clue to the Mystery.

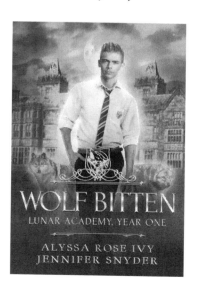

Four Houses. Traditions. Secrets. And Romance Waiting At Every Turn. Welcome to Lunar Academy. Which House Will You Choose?

Tori Ballard chose to become a wolf. For as long as she could remember it was something she'd wanted. The problem: her wolf is impulsive and free-spirited. She relies on instincts and not much else, which isn't how Tori moves through life. She prefers structure, schedules, and knowing things well in advance. Until she decides to give in to the sexy southern guy fate seems to be forcing her way.

Holt Taylor had a solid plan for his life until it evaporated when he was attacked and bitten. Now he's part wolf and enrolled at the academy. He still feels angry, lost, and as though he's spiraling. There are only a few things that can put him back on solid ground–fight club, cardio, and Tori. Even if she doesn't know it yet.

When the two find themselves pulled into something bigger than anything they've ever been a part of, they must focus on their future while trying to contain the passion brewing between them.

Available now!

Printed in Great Britain
by Amazon